HAPPILY MARRIED

BOOKS BY VICTORIA JENKINS

The Divorce

The Argument

The Accusation

The Playdate

The New Family

The Bridesmaids

The Midwife

DETECTIVES KING AND LANE SERIES

The Girls in the Water

The First One to Die

Nobody's Child

A Promise to the Dead

HAPPILY MARRIED

VICTORIA JENKINS

bookouture

Published by Bookouture in 2023

An imprint of Storyfire Ltd.
Carmelite House
50 Victoria Embankment
London EC4Y 0DZ

www.bookouture.com

ISBN: 978-1-83790-240-8
eBook ISBN: 978-1-83790-239-2

For Steve – who came to stay for a week and never left

PROLOGUE

She doesn't realise there's anyone else in the house. As far as she knows, it's just her and the silence, the echoes of their earlier argument only just faded. She should get out of here now, while she's got a chance, and yet the same fear hangs over her. There's nowhere for her to go. Wherever she goes, she'll be found.

It's then she hears the creak. An old floorboard. A footstep.

She goes to the bedroom door and eases it open. She waits there, listening, her body braced. Nothing but silence. She waits a while longer. There's no one here. She feels her chest lighten, a weight of anticipation exhaled. She goes out onto the landing. Perhaps she'll leave now. There's still time.

But there isn't time. Everything happens so suddenly she doesn't have time to react. A movement behind her. Hands on her back. The shove comes so hard she isn't able to steady herself or break the fall. She hits the banister first, then the wall, pinballing down the staircase. Her head cracks against the corner of the hallway table. And then there is only silence again.

PART ONE

ONE

Natalie closes the laptop as Jake comes back from the barn, rain-soaked and shivering. He kicks off his wellies and leaves them in the porch by the kitchen door. She grabs a tea towel and passes it to him, watching as he wipes the water from his face. A beautiful face, she thinks. Dark eyes, weather-kissed skin, thick hair that needs cutting; a strong jaw peppered with stubble. His face suits their landscape.

He barely acknowledges her before going to the sink to wash his hands, his eyes weighted with tiredness; his mind presumably distracted, as hers is, by the possibility of another outbreak of illness among the cattle.

'How is she?' Natalie asks.

'Tyler's with the vet now. Everything okay?'

For a moment, she thinks he's asking after her – an expression of concern rarely offered these days. Then she realises he's referring to the laptop and to what she'd been doing when he'd come in.

'Fine. Just catching up on some emails.' She pushes her unruly hair from her face, an awkward gesture that betrays the white lie. She isn't fine, though it's not her he's interested in. His thoughts seem to lie solely with the farm these days. She's barely slept in three nights, worry keeping her awake while all her fears stood at their bedside looking worse in the darkness. Elsie has seemed lethargic again these past few days, which always reignites her anxiety. The end of the summer season has brought with it the anticipated drought in ice cream sales, and knowing it was on its way hasn't made them any more prepared for the financial hit. Jake is distracted. The same can be said for her. They should probably talk more, she thinks, but with life as it is there never seems to be the right time or place. There never seems to be any space for saying what they're feeling.

'Do you want something to eat?'

She goes to him, puts her hands around his waist and rests her head on his shoulder, waiting for his response.

'No, thanks.'

He moves away, and she feels the rejection like a burn.

'Not interrupting anything, am I?'

She hadn't heard Tyler at the door. He stands in the porchway, his wellies caked in mud. The rain has been relentless for hours, the mood of the place as dark as the evening sky that hangs heavy over the farm. It's forecast to rain solidly for another two days.

'The vet's just left,' he tells them. 'He doesn't seem overly concerned. Reckons another lot of antibiotics should sort it.'

Natalie feels relief swell in her stomach. Last year, they'd lost two-thirds of their cattle when the herd had been struck by bovine TB. It had almost broken them. They can't afford for anything else to happen.

'Have Peppa and George been fed?' she asks. She bought the two piglets earlier in the year, with a plan to rear them to breed – an additional way to make some extra income. That plan changed when Elsie fell in love with them both, and now they're more like the family pets than farm animals.

'I've just done it,' Tyler tells her.

'Thank you. I'd better go and check on Elsie.' She goes up to her daughter's room every evening to check on her, sometimes as many as three or four times before going to bed. Sometimes she sits on the carpet by her bed for a while and watches the rhythmic rise and fall of her chest beneath her nightdress; other times, she will gently lift her clothing to check her body for signs of a rash.

A raging headache pulses at her temples. When she goes upstairs, she stops first at the bathroom, where she takes a packet of painkillers from the cupboard. When she goes to Elsie's room, she finds her wound within the duvet. Natalie doesn't move her; she looks peaceful as she is, her left arm raised above her head, her right leg bent at the knee like a ballet dancer frozen in a sleeping pirouette. She's nearly three and a half, yet she seems far younger, small for her age and delayed in her speech – just another thing for Natalie to worry about.

When she goes back downstairs, Tyler has gone. Jake is sitting at the table eating a piece of toast, despite having rejected her offer to make him something. He gets up and goes to the sink, takes a glass from the draining board and fills it with water. Natalie's focus is captured by the softness of his lips as he drains the drink. She tries to remember when she last kissed him, or when he last tried to instigate any sort of intimacy with her. She can't recall either.

'Tyler seemed quite relaxed about things,' she says, desperate for something to break the silence.

Jake runs a hand over his face. 'I trust the vet's judgement. Try not to overthink it.'

As if it's that easy, she thinks. As if after everything the past eighteen months has thrown at them, she should be more optimistic.

She watches his back as he flicks on the kettle and takes two mugs from the cupboard. He doesn't want to say what either of them is thinking, that they can't afford to lose another animal, yet the unspoken burden hangs silently in the air between them, an invisible threat that keeps them from any sense of peace.

'Have you thought any more about my suggestion?'

For weeks now, Natalie has been talking about the idea of renting out the farmhouse's spare bedroom. It isn't used for anything – decades ago planned for the second child Natalie's parents never had – and it makes sense to her that the space should be used to help boost their waning income. They're outdoors a lot of the time, the farm requiring labour that doesn't fit within a nine-to-five routine; a lodger would have plenty of privacy, and they would in turn be able to keep theirs.

Jake presses his palms against the worktop as he waits for the kettle to boil. 'I don't know. I'm still not sure how I feel about having a stranger in the house.' He turns to her now, looking at her for the first time since coming into the kitchen. 'How do we know it's safe for Elsie?'

'We'll get references. Loads of families do it now – there's no danger if we check everything thoroughly. We can be specific about the type of person we want. You've always been a good judge of character. You'll know soon enough whether you like the person or not.'

'What type of person *would* we want?'

Natalie has given this plenty of thought. Female, definitely female. She doesn't really mind what age, but nobody too young; not younger than they are. A professional, preferably, although what kind of professional would move to their part of the country to rent a room on an isolated farmhouse she isn't sure. How a potential future lodger makes her money is less important to Natalie than that she actually makes it and can pay the rent – within reason, she supposes.

The kettle clicks off, the water boiled, and Jake turns to make them tea. Natalie realises her answers have all been confined to her head, and her lack of response has managed to fuel his doubts. 'I just don't see why anyone would want to live here.' His words are cutting.

'Thanks a lot,' she mutters.

'Come on, you know what I mean. We live in the arse end of nowhere.'

Years ago there had been dreams of other places and different things, but a single morning had torn their world apart, keeping them tethered to the stretch of countryside in which they'd both grown up. There were times Natalie lamented still being here, wondering what life might have offered had she ventured beyond this strip of land that's defined her life, yet when she considers everything, she thinks them lucky to be here. They have a home that's paid for and land that earns their living, just about. There is space for their daughter to run and roam safely; she will have the same countryside childhood they both lived and loved. They are safe. They have the security of each other.

'Which might be some people's idea of heaven,' she counteracts. 'Plenty of people work remotely now. And loads of people are escaping city life for the country – it's becoming more and more popular, apparently. We've got beautiful walks, fresh air, endless countryside. We're the antidote to twenty-first-century living.'

Jake smiles wryly as he goes to the fridge for milk. 'Is that how you plan to word the advertisement?'

'Maybe.' The chair legs scrape across the tiled floor as Natalie stands to get a pen and paper from a drawer. 'Come on,' she says, gesturing for Jake to join her at the table. 'We can word it together. I don't want to be responsible for something you're not happy with.'

She returns to the table and opens the notebook, and together they begin to plan what they want to write. He passes her a mug and sits next to her; they nurse their tea as they deliberate over semantics, and with a swell of sadness, Natalie realises that apart from when they've been sleeping or arguing, this is the closest they have been to one another in as long as she's able to remember. Unlike earlier, he hasn't moved away.

Twenty minutes after starting the advertisement, Natalie sits back and assesses their efforts.

> *Spacious double bedroom available to a female happy to share a home with a young family in a farmhouse set in 500 acres of land, amid beautiful countryside. Our family lives on a working dairy farm, from where we also run an ice cream/coffee shop and children's play area. We are looking for someone professional but fun-loving who will fit in with our busy family life – someone who likes children and doesn't mind the smell of manure.*

'Do you think we should add at the end that we're referring to the cows and not to Elsie?' Natalie jokes.

Jakes smiles, but it is only half an effort. He still doesn't want to go ahead with this, she thinks. Circumstances have backed him into a corner.

'Good to go?' she asks.

Jake nods, his reluctance obvious. She reaches across the table and takes his hand, silently willing him not to let go. When his fingers close tightly around hers, she feels her heart lighten.

'Thank you. I'll make this work, I promise.'

Once they've found the right person and he realises the financial benefits far outweigh his concerns, Natalie's sure Jake will change his mind. A fresh face around the place might be good for them all. This could turn out to be the best decision they've ever made. With a click of a button, Natalie uploads the advertisement. She breathes an inward sigh of relief, hoping a new chapter of their lives is about to begin.

TWO

Mum is at the window in the conservatory, sitting looking out at the long, narrow garden of the terraced house she's lived in all my life. It's overgrown, left to grow wild, the vast trellis that runs almost the whole length of the lawn now barely visible beyond the brambles that have staked their claim to the land. Dad was the gardener, and he'd cultivated the project for over a decade. I don't think Mum knows one end of a rosebush from the other.

'Do you want me to do a bit of weeding?' I offer, though a bit of weeding wouldn't really begin to resolve the mess the place has become.

'No. You've got enough to be doing. Thanks, though.'

What Mum really means is that she doesn't want me to touch it. The garden was Dad's territory; since he's been gone, she hasn't wanted to change anything. The whole house has become a shrine to the past, my mother Miss Havisham in a tartan dressing gown. She should get out more: she works from home, she orders most of her shopping to the house, and she cut ties with the few remaining friends she had years ago. She doesn't listen to me though. She never has.

I put the tea on the table beneath the window and sit down in one of the wicker chairs that've been here since I was a kid. 'I miss him.'

'I know.'

We don't really talk about Dad much. I'd like to more, but every time I mention him, she changes the subject. It's a skill she's managed to perfect.

'You working today?'

And just like that, he's gone again, the thought of him melded among the humdrum conversation of everyday life, a passing comment amid a hundred others that will be passed throughout the day. I hate it when she does this, how she's able to just turn herself off from the memory of him. I clench a fist and try to push back the anger that surges through me. It's easier to control some days than others.

'Morning off,' I lie. The truth is, I can't be bothered. There's plenty I could be doing, but I'm too distracted by what I saw this morning to think of anything except Jake and the lies he's spun me. At the thought of it, I take my phone from my pocket. I took a screenshot of the advertisement I found on the 'Find Me a Room' website and I return to it now, holding the phone out for Mum to take from me.

'Look at this. Why would he want a stranger to move in with them?'

'This is Jake?' Mum finishes reading the advertisement and purses her lips. 'The extra income? That's usually why people rent out a spare room.'

I know things haven't been going too well for them at the farm, but Jake hasn't given any suggestion that they're so bad they've considered renting a room out to a lodger. Perhaps this is all Natalie's idea and she's managed to persuade him to agree. Or maybe Jake came up with the idea, hoping to somehow distract from what he surely now must know is imminent. Either way, the advertisement burned as though a direct message was being carried to me: he isn't going anywhere. I've been waiting for something that's never going to happen.

Mum passes the phone back to me. 'How do you feel about it?'

I shrug. I'm crushed, but I can't tell her that. She doesn't approve of our relationship, or at the least she doesn't approve of the fact he's married. She drops the odd sly comment in here and there sometimes, taking pleasure in reminding me that I'm the dirty secret.

'He's obviously not going to leave her,' I say.

'Not necessarily. Maybe he's hoping to get her some company before he tells her. Soften the blow a bit so she doesn't have to stay there alone. Jake isn't a cruel man, is he? You wouldn't be holding out for him if he was.'

Holding out for him. It makes me sound so desperate, like some sort of lovesick teenager obsessed with an older man – the kind of idiot who might be picked up and discarded again on the whim of a husband in the midst of some sort of crisis. But I suppose that's exactly what I am. The bit on the side.

'How did you know Dad was the one?'

My mother laughs awkwardly. 'God, there's a question. I don't know.'

The sun struggles beyond the weeping willows at the bottom of the garden as the nonchalance of her response settles like fog around us. I wonder what Jake is doing now. He might be outside on the farm, tending to the cattle. He might be at the house, drinking tea with his wife. Maybe he's getting ready to take Elsie to nursery. Wherever he is and whatever he's doing, I can't escape the sting that it should be me there doing those things with him.

'I think the idea of "the one" is a bit misleading though, love,' Mum says. 'Think of the millions of people in the world. No one would ever have a chance of bumping into *the* one, would they? Life is hard. Relationships are hard. You have to work at it.' She raises an eyebrow. 'And your dad was a single man,' she adds.

She may not approve, but she knows our circumstances are far from usual. Jake loves me: I know it. It's only fear of the unknown that's stopping him from being with me. He doesn't know how to break free from his life, and if he can't bring himself to make the leap then maybe he needs someone to give him a push.

'He doesn't love her.'

'But that's for him to decide.'

I've lost count of how many times Jake's told me he's going to leave Natalie, but there's always some excuse: circumstances aren't right at the farm; he'll lose access to his daughter; Natalie's mental health is bad again, and he just can't do it to her.

I'm starting to think he's never going to do it. Not without some encouragement, at least.

'What are you going to do?' Mum asks.

I knew from the first time we met there would be something between Jake and me. He tried to hide it, but I saw how he looked at me – I could see in his eyes the way he'd one day look at me, once I'd made him mine. For a long time, he tried to bury his feelings for me, as though they might eventually die if he was able to suppress them for long enough. But what we've got is too strong for that. Jake's place is with me, and there is nothing I won't do to make him mine.

'Whatever I need to,' I tell her.

THREE

Less than a week after putting out their advertisement for a lodger, Natalie and Jake receive interest from three people. The first is a man who apparently has ignored the detail that they're looking for a female lodger, and the second is someone known to them, a woman from the village who was a couple of years above them in school and is in the process of going through a divorce. She is too familiar, they decide. They need someone neutral and previously unknown to them; someone who won't bring trouble to their door. There are rumours the woman's husband was violent, and the last thing they'd want is him showing up at the farm.

The third person to respond to their advertisement is a woman named Kara Barton. Natalie sees the email first and checks her out online, finding a closed Facebook page and Instagram account also set to private. Her profile pictures show a woman around the age of thirty. She's pretty in an understated way, with light red hair cut mid-length and unusually coloured green eyes that Natalie suspects may be contact lenses. Her smile's natural and there's something about her that even through a photograph radiates warmth. She wonders what job she does, presuming something from home. She emails her back. Would she like to come to the farm for an informal chat? They are free on Thursday afternoon if she's able to make it then.

Natalie closes down the laptop and goes outside. She's been so distracted by their potential future lodger that she hadn't heard the vet's car pull onto the driveway, and when she goes into the barn he's there with Jake and Tyler, tending to the cow he's been treating for the past week.

'How is she?'

'It's definitely mastitis,' the vet says. 'One of the worst cases I've seen, though.' He runs a hand along the animal's back before standing. 'But thankfully for you, nothing worse. She's stronger than she was last time I came. I'm going to extend the course of antibiotics just to be on the safe side.'

Natalie goes to the cow and puts a hand on its face, staying with her while Jake and Tyler follow the vet outside. 'You'll be okay, girl,' she says soothingly, stroking the curve of the cow's back. 'Everything works itself out in the end.'

That evening, with the two of them barely having crossed paths again during the day, she forgets to tell Jake that Kara will be visiting the farm on Thursday. By the time he finishes his paperwork that evening, Natalie has already gone to bed, nursing the headache that plagued her all afternoon and refused to be eased with painkillers. She hears him on the stairs and listens when he goes to the bathroom, waiting for him to come to bed. Instead, he goes back downstairs, and when Natalie wakes at nearly midnight, a gale at the window rousing her from sleep, he still isn't there, presumably having fallen asleep on the sofa again.

The following morning, when Natalie tells Jake about their potential new lodger, he reacts with an apathy that riles her. His lack of interest extends itself to Thursday, by which time he seems to have either forgotten or decided not to make any mention of Kara, as though hoping silence will make the prospect of a lodger disappear altogether.

'You'd better go and make yourself presentable,' Natalie says when he returns to the house at lunchtime. 'Our potential new lodger will be here soon.'

She watches his face as he goes to wash his hands. There's a flicker of a reaction at his jaw, a tightening around his mouth, but his dark eyes remain focused on his hands and he doesn't so much as turn to look at her, not bothering to acknowledge her words with a response.

'We need the money,' she reminds him quietly. Like Jake, she wishes it wasn't the case. This is their family home and inviting a stranger in isn't a prospect she's taken lightly.

He turns back to look at her.

'I've made you a sandwich,' she says, gesturing to the plate near the microwave.

'Thanks. Where's Elsie?'

'Having a nap.'

'Not like her.'

'She had a bad night,' Natalie tells him, resentful that his own sleep hadn't been disturbed enough to have even noticed Elsie had woken.

Her attention reverts back to the laptop where she searches the name Kara Barton again, returning to her Facebook and Instagram profile pictures.

'This is her,' Natalie says, turning the laptop so Jake can see the screen.

He fills a glass with water at the sink and barely glances over his shoulder to look. He takes his sandwich through to the living room and eats it there while Natalie goes upstairs to check her hair and make-up. She wants to make a good first impression, though whoever moves into the spare room will quickly see that her efforts today are far from typical. Life on the farm leaves little time or energy for being too concerned by her appearance.

Natalie sees Kara get out from her car. She looks younger in person than she does in her online photographs, and her hair is brighter, recently coloured a warm red. Even from this distance her skin looks unblemished. Alabaster. She is pretty, Natalie thinks, and the thought is accompanied by a flutter of uncertainty that skips through her stomach, evaporating when she dismisses it as juvenile.

She pauses to straighten her hair at the mirror in the hallway, pulling her ponytail a little higher and wiping the corners of her eyes to realign the eyeliner she applied earlier. First impressions count, she thinks – hers as much as Kara's.

She opens the door before Kara has a chance to knock, greeting her with a smile and a welcome to the farm. She is quietly spoken and polite, her accent neutral, and when she follows Natalie through to the living room she looks cautiously around her, silently absorbing the details of the place.

Natalie feels a flush of shame at how old-fashioned the house still is. She's wanted to renovate it for years, but there's never been the time or the money. Over the space of a decade she's got around to changing the curtains and the soft furnishings, but the fading carpet has been here since her parents were alive and the paintwork is in desperate need of refreshing.

'Can I get you something to drink?' she offers. 'A tea or a coffee?'

'Tea would be lovely, thanks.'

'Milk and sugar?'

'Just milk. I suppose there's no chance of you ever running out of that here.' She laughs at her own joke, the sound a nervous titter that manages to expel itself too loudly.

She's as self-conscious as I am, Natalie thinks, and the notion offers a reassurance that helps her relax.

'Wouldn't be much of a dairy farm then, would it? Make

yourself comfortable, and I won't be long. I'll try to find where
Elsie's gone... she's been looking forward to meeting you.'

The latter is a lie: Natalie told Elsie they were having a
visitor that afternoon, but her daughter barely batted an eyelid
and has shown no interest. Perhaps she'll be different after her
nap. Natalie has wondered how the presence of someone else in
the house might affect her, but Elsie is such a laid-back child
that she seems to take everything in her stride. Give it a week,
Natalie thinks, and it will seem to Elsie as though Kara's always
been here.

As the tea brews, Elsie wanders into the kitchen. Her
clothing is stained with the lunch she ate before she fell asleep,
a long trail of gravy lining her sweater like a third, ungainly
strap of the dungaree dress that sits over it. Her hair is dishevelled, the French plait Natalie had styled for her earlier now
loosened with strands that stick out from her head like a scare-
crow's. There's no time to do anything about her appearance
now, and Natalie smiles at the thought: she is perfect just as she
is, no change needed. Kara is going to have to take them as they
are, gravy stains and all.

'Hey,' Natalie says. 'Are you feeling better now?'

Elsie mumbles a response before following Natalie into the
living room, clinging to her mother's leg as she manoeuvres to
put Kara's cup of tea on the coffee table.

'Elsie,' she coaxes, crouching to meet her daughter at eye
level. 'This is Kara. Are you going to say hello?'

She is silent as she peers around Natalie's hip. Kara gives
her a wave and a smile before introducing herself. 'Hi, Elsie. I'm
Kara. It's lovely to meet you.'

Elsie giggles and runs out of the living room.

'Apologies,' Natalie says. 'She's always shy around anyone
new.'

'Well, she's right not to talk to strangers.' She smiles, and
there's an awkward moment of silence that for Natalie is filled

only with her own anxiety. Where is Jake? He promised he'd be here before Kara arrived, but she hasn't seen him since she gave him his lunch. If he doesn't make an appearance she's going to have to do this on her own, and if he's happy to absolve himself of the responsibility of interviewing their potential lodger then she'll assume by his absence that he's also prepared to leave her with the sole decision of who is chosen.

Natalie sits in the chair opposite Kara, who sits at the end of the sofa, her slim hand resting on its arm. 'So what brings you to us?' she asks. 'We're quite remote and very rural. It wouldn't be everyone's cup of tea.'

'It's got a certain charm. I've been looking for somewhere quiet. This place seems perfect.'

'I guessed that might be the case. We're the antidote to the rat race.' She smiles awkwardly. 'Jake should be here soon.'

As though hearing himself mentioned, he appears at the living room doorway.

Kara turns to him. 'Hi,' she says, her face fixed with a smile. 'I'm Kara.'

Jake stares at her, unresponsive. His temple twitches. 'Natalie. Can I have a word a minute.'

She feels a rush of heat rise in her chest as she gets up from the chair. What the hell is Jake playing at, being so rude to this woman? She can't remember ever seeing him behaving so ignorantly towards somebody, and she feels herself smarting with something she realises is bigger than embarrassment. Disappointment. Kara will write their family off before Natalie's so much as had a chance to show her around the house.

She pulls the door behind her as she leaves the living room, careful not to close it fully. She doesn't want Kara to feel herself shut out – or worse, closed in – though neither does she want her to overhear whatever it is Jake wants to say.

'What's the matter with you?' she whispers. 'Why are you acting so weird?'

The vein at Jake's temple throbs. 'You said she was around our age. She looks a lot younger.'

Natalie raises her hands in frustration. 'That's it? So what? Perhaps she just looks young for her age. Lucky her.' She shakes her head. 'Are you coming, then? Please, just keep an open mind.'

When they go back into the room, Kara is sitting with her head turned to the window.

'Sorry,' Natalie says breezily, as though Jake's weirdness hasn't just happened. 'We're having a problem with one of the cows.'

'Oh. Poor thing.' As she speaks, Kara's bright eyes follow Jake as he sits at the opposite end of the sofa. She smiles at him with perfect teeth, but he continues to distract himself, avoiding having to look at her.

'I was just asking Kara why she chose this place,' Natalie tells him, forcing a smile she knows must look as fake as it feels. Jake looks as though he's just received a particularly unpleasant tax bill.

'You've got a lovely home,' Kara says, her eyes still resting on Jake. 'So much character. How long have you lived here?'

'I grew up here,' Natalie explains. 'Jake and I have been together since school.'

Jake shifts awkwardly and picks at the nail of his right thumb, a habit that's always irritated Natalie. It starts whenever he's feeling anxious or frustrated by something, though in their current situation she sees no reason why he should be either. Kara seems lovely, and nothing has been agreed between them anyway; today is just a chat, so what exactly is his problem?

'Childhood sweethearts,' Kara says. 'That's so romantic.'

If only that were the case, Natalie thinks. She glances at Jake, who still hasn't looked up from his hands. Now, his left leg is jiggling as though he's got some kind of tremor; it's so distracting she wants to reach over and grip his knee to stop it.

'You must be the envy of the town,' Kara adds. 'Beautiful home... beautiful family. You really are living the dream.'

'You're very kind,' Natalie replies. 'But I don't think they envy us the smell of manure.' She laughs nervously at her own joke, feeling the heat of Jake's disapproval on the side of her face. 'So what do you do for work? I'm guessing you must work from home?'

Kara nods. 'For the past couple of years,' she tells them. 'You know, since working from home became the new normal.' She pulls a face. 'I hate that phrase. I work in IT. I'm a software developer. It's as boring as it sounds. I don't mind working from home though. I quite like my own company. I wouldn't get under your feet or anything. I should have asked in my email, but do you get a decent internet connection here?'

Natalie nods. 'We couldn't keep the business going without it.'

Jake's staring at the fireplace. The vein at his temple writhes like a worm beneath his skin. 'This place is boring,' he says abruptly, the first words he's spoken since entering the room. 'I mean, you're young; there's no nightlife of any description around here.'

'Not really my scene,' Kara replies. 'I prefer a quiet night in.'

'Me too,' Natalie says. 'Probably just as well though... Jake's right, there's nothing to do around here unless you fancy drinking with the regulars at the Red Lion, and I can tell you from experience that they could talk a glass eye to sleep—' She's rambling, and when she notices the way Jake looks at her, she cuts herself short. An uncomfortable silence settles over them.

'We're not really selling it here, are we?' she says with an awkward laugh. 'Tell us a bit about yourself, Kara, to help us get to know you.'

'Well, I'm twenty-nine. I'm an only child. I studied law for a while at university but it wasn't meant to be, and then I ended up working in IT.' She pauses for a moment to sip her tea. 'I lost my dad earlier this year. It's made me look at things differently. Life is short, isn't it? We've got to take our chances when they come. Take what we want when we can.'

'I'm sorry about your dad.'

Natalie feels Jake's gaze upon the side of her face. He knows how sensitive she is to these conversations.

'He'd been unwell for quite a while, so it wasn't a shock when he went. It didn't make it any easier, though.'

Silence settles over them again, none of them sure what to say to break it.

'I'm sorry,' Kara says. 'I didn't mean to be maudlin.'

'You're not. I asked you to share something, so thank you for being honest. Would you like to have a look around? We could show you the house and the garden. You'll be pleased to hear it's not all barns and milking machines.'

There's movement at the living room door. Natalie is glad to see Tyler there, so all the introductions can be done at once. 'This is Tyler,' she tells Kara. 'We grew up together, went to the same school – our parents were friends. Now he works with us on the farm. He's practically family, aren't you? This is Kara.'

Tyler runs a hand across the stubble he's recently left to grow longer. Natalie notices him take in the details of her face, and she wonders if he finds Kara attractive. They'd look good together, she thinks, and it's about time he found someone.

'Nice to meet you, Kara. Sorry to interrupt... Jake, I need a hand with something.'

Jake can't leave quickly enough; so much so that Natalie wonders whether he set Tyler up to come in here and give him an excuse to leave. Whatever he apparently needed a hand with, Tyler wasn't specific about it.

Stop being so suspicious, she berates herself. It isn't like her to think badly of people, and she doesn't like the way it makes her feel, particularly when the thoughts are of her own husband.

'Come on,' she says with a smile, gesturing for Kara to follow her. 'I'll find Elsie and we'll show you around the place. She can introduce you to Peppa and George. Hopefully you'll love it here as much as we do.'

'I'm sure I will,' Kara says, following Natalie to the living room door. 'Are they your parents?'

Natalie feels a coldness seep through her skin, as though a ghost has just passed through her. Then she follows Kara's gaze to the photograph on the bookcase in the corner. 'Yes.'

'It must have been hard staying here.'

Natalie says nothing, but she hears the end of Kara's sentence without her having to speak it. *After what happened.* But how does Kara know? Natalie hasn't mentioned anything, not even after Kara mentioned her own father's death. It's nothing, she tells herself. Her history can be found online by anyone who might want to look for it, and perhaps Kara has taken as much time to find out about her as she has to find out about Kara.

'Come on,' she says, keen to find her coat and expel the chill from her bones. 'Follow me.'

FOUR

It is late evening. The farm lies quiet and peaceful, the cold weight of the October air holding the place still beneath its grip. I wait at the boundary of the farm, watching as it settles for the night. My senses are alive with the place, its sounds and smells: the thick evening air that touches its fingertips to my skin; the cracks and rustles that whisper from the hedgerow running around the farm's front entrance. The farm has its own kind of unique beauty – a rough-around-the-edges, unkempt charm that's different to anything I've ever known before. Surrounding the farmhouse itself is an old stone wall that divides the front and back gardens from the adjoining fields. From it I can see the start of the barns and the milking sheds, the pigsty in the lower field, and to the left of the house is the old converted double garage that now serves as the coffee and ice cream shop, temporarily closed for the winter months. The children's play area lies to the left just beyond it, the silhouettes of its equipment standing like metal monsters in the darkness.

There are pumpkins placed at the front door, their jagged mouths and triangular eyes lit by the soft glow of the outside light. The rest of the place is steeped in darkness, and the house looks so different at this time of night, as everything does. There's a supernatural quality to it, aided by the decorations Natalie's hung from the trees – ghosts and bats that flap in the breeze, swaying like dead birds trapped in the branches. But there is also a romance to the place; something mysterious that can't be captured by a single word. It's the setting of a nineteenth-century novel; it's an oil painting faded with age and neglect. Natalie clearly doesn't have a clue what to do with the place to modernise it in a way that would be sympathetic to its original features, but with the right expertise and someone who knows what they're doing it could be made into a beautiful home, worth far more than it is now. I understand why someone might not want to leave here. I understand why Jake's so tied to it.

Winter is beginning its slow creep upon the land, the fields damp with dew that settles on the grass and sparkles like diamonds beneath the moonlight. The fields beyond the barns stretch into the darkness. Five hundred acres of farmland punctuated by trees and hedgerow. The place is beautiful, but it could be perfect given a chance. Given the right person.

I go through the large wooden gate and tread carefully along the gravel driveway, not wanting to make any noise and draw attention to myself. Downstairs, the curtains are all shut for the evening, but upstairs they're still open, and a soft glow pours from what must be a light left on in the landing or bathroom, presumably in case Elsie wakes up during the night.

There is movement at the bedroom window. I step aside to keep myself concealed in the shadows and press my body to the side of Jake's van, from where I can continue to watch unseen. I've lost count of the number of times we've had sex in the back of this van. It was exciting, at first – there was a danger to it, the fear that we might get caught or be seen adding to the tension that's always hung between us like static. He'd begin to remove my clothes before we'd managed to get the door closed behind us, our urgency in those early days so immediate that neither of us could wait to taste the other.

The thought of those encounters sends a thrill through me. It's been weeks since I was last able to touch him, but I plan to do something about that soon. As the thought moves through my mind, there's movement in the upstairs window. Jake and Natalie's bedroom. I stand poised, still fearful I might be seen out here, but I can't keep my eyes from the window, waiting as Jake appears in view. He's wearing the same checked shirt he had on earlier, and I watch as he unbuttons it, catching a flash of his exposed chest before he turns away from the window. Outdoor living has kept his body taut and lean; the lifestyle suits him. He belongs to this place.

He disappears from sight for a moment; when he returns, he's changed into a T-shirt. His hair is unruly, dishevelled. I imagine running my hands through it, there upstairs with him in the bedroom. Me instead of her. The thought of Natalie throws a grenade through my fantasy, blasting it to pieces. Blood pounds in my ears. It should be me up in that bedroom, in that bed. I feel my jaw tighten as Jake nears the windows and closes the curtains, a pain so sharp and cutting it feels as though it could be real tearing through me as he shuts me outside in the cold, left here alone.

I picture Jake in the bedroom, sliding beneath the duvet beside his wife's soft, pale body. Images I don't want to have to see grow stronger as I try to force them back: Natalie's thighs straddling his legs; her mouth exploring the contours of his lean body. I wonder how often he's expected to make love to her; how often he's forced to fake a pleasure I know he can't possibly feel when he's alone with her. He's told me they rarely have sex any more, but I'm not naïve enough to unquestioningly accept it as the truth. How could she not want him? How could anyone not want him?

I wait until the bedroom light is turned off and then I go

around the side of the house and into one of the barns where the cows lie sleeping. The animals are beautiful in their own way, strong and imposing. Their black and white bodies rise and fall with their breathing, though I realise now they're not all asleep. One looks at me questioningly, its bright eyes shining in the darkness. It seems to realise I shouldn't be out here with them at this time of night, as though it knows something's wrong. It recognises me as a danger.

These animals mean the world to Jake and Natalie. All their life is in this place: their history, their income; their future. The thought stirs a restlessness in me that I'm usually able to quell. I could make all this disappear. One decision, one lit match, and I could watch their life disintegrate around them. I could start a fire and watch everything burn. The security that holds Jake to this place would be gone. Without the farm, would he leave her? Perhaps it's just this place that's keeping him from being with me?

FIVE

On Friday night, Natalie arrives home from work just before 10.30 p.m. The second job she took on at a local gastro pub a few weeks ago is already starting to take its toll. She is grateful to the landlord: he knows she only intends to stay until the end of February when she'll be ready to reopen the ice cream shop, yet he has still employed her to work in their kitchen for three evenings a week. She is enjoying it more than she'd expected to, but the late evenings and anti-social hours are making her more tired than she'd anticipated.

The pub's a mile and a half away, most of it down the country lanes that lead to the village. She could take the car but she chooses not to: she likes the night air, and the exercise is a change from her usual daily activity of chasing after Elsie and running errands around the farm. The village is so quiet that there's no one around at night, and the lanes barely see any cars after dark. As she returns to the gravel driveway and walks around the side of the farmhouse, Natalie sees the kitchen light is on. There's movement at the table; she sees Jake gesticulating animatedly at whoever sits opposite.

As she nears, she sees Tyler. He's sitting opposite Jake at the table, his face stern, his eyes narrowed in concentration. There's something open in front of them, a folder spilling paperwork between their mugs. When she opens the back door, Jake swipes the sheets away, gathering them into a pile and returning them to the folder.

'Everything okay?' she asks. 'You're here late.'

Not for the first time recently, she wonders what Jake's hiding from her. He's tried to protect her from their financial problems before, but she's not a child and she doesn't want to be treated like one.

'Good news,' Tyler says, his grey eyes shooting Jake a look. 'Go on. You tell her.'

'We've had a response from Adler's,' Jake tells her. 'They want to try your ice cream.'

It's a small retail chain but getting their brand into any shop would be a stepping stone to gaining interest from the larger national supermarkets. Natalie knows she should be excited by the news.

'Could be an ongoing relationship if you manage to secure a contract,' Tyler adds. 'We should be celebrating.' His chair scrapes across the tiled floor as he pushes it back.

'Did Elsie go off okay?' she asks.

'Fine,' Jake tells her. 'She was exhausted, fell asleep by seven-fifteen.' He nods when Tyler pulls a beer from the fridge and waves the bottle at him. As far as Natalie's concerned, any celebrations are premature. There's a long winter ahead of them, and a contract with Adler's would only scratch the surface of their financial problems.

Besides that, she does her best to avoid drink. The antidepressants she has taken since her parents' deaths almost a decade earlier shouldn't be mixed with alcohol, and though she sometimes misses how it feels to let her hair down, she doesn't dare stop taking the medication. She's relied on it for so long now that she fears her own behaviour if she stops. She no longer knows who she is without it.

When Tyler leans over to pass Jake an opened bottle of beer, the kitchen light catches the deep scar that follows the curve of his sharp cheekbone, and for a moment Natalie's mind is wrenched back in time. The memory of that day plays out as though it is all happening in front of her, still too alive and unfaded by time. She was eighteen years old and a couple of months off sitting her final A level exams. She'd been predicted two A grades and a B, with Nottingham University having already made an unconditional offer of a place to study History of Art. It was a wet April day; she'd watched from the Art class-room as a relentless downpour battered the windowpane. She remembers the piece she was working on: an oil painting of a rotten pear, its browning flesh split like a wound, the inner fruit pulped and shining. Later, she'd burn it, along with the uniform she'd been wearing and the bag she'd carried as she'd followed the head teacher to his office, already knowing somehow in her heart why he'd gone there to call her from her lesson.

'Are you okay, Nat?' Tyler snaps her back to the present. He's returned to his seat at the table and is watching her, concern etched alongside his scar.

'What are they offering?'

This is the first time they'll have tried to sell the ice cream beyond the farm. The shop only opened its doors last year, though Natalie was experimenting with ice cream production for a while before that. After selling at local events, she persuaded Jake to agree to the garage conversion. Until then, it was used for storing junk, and they have plenty of other available storage. They had to take out a loan to get the renovation work done and the place kitted out with all the equipment needed, but Natalie believed she could make it work. Jake remains unconvinced, put off by the absence of any footfall passing the farm. She realises she's got a lot to prove.

'I can take some sample flavours to pitch next week,' Jake tells her. 'If they like it, they'll make us an offer then.'

'It's good news, Nat,' Tyler says, eyebrows raised in persuasion.

'You're right. Thank you,' she says to Jake. 'And go on then,' she adds, turning her attention to Tyler. 'I'll join you. One beer won't hurt.'

Jake eyes her warily as she accepts a beer from Tyler, but she dismisses his doubts with a shrug. 'I'm fine,' she mutters, and when she puts a hand on his arm she can't help but notice him flinch beneath her touch. Did she imagine it? she wonders. She's tired from work and it's been a long day; perhaps she's being overly sensitive.

Natalie clinks the top of her bottle against Tyler's when he holds it out to her. She extends the gesture to Jake. 'To us,' she says. He clinks his bottle against hers, but he doesn't return the gesture, and she feels the sting of it like a physical wound.

Natalie distracts herself with positive thoughts. If they can secure this deal with Adler's and earn a reputation for her product, it will only lead on to more interest. This could be the start of something great for them. And on Monday, Kara will be moving in. She had confirmation that morning that she wants to accept their offer of the room. Amid all the family's ongoing financial problems, her arrival offers the hope of a fresh start. Kara seems like she'll be a calming influence, and she's around the same age as Natalie. Who knows – perhaps she and Kara may even become friends. It will be nice to have someone to talk to.

SIX

On Monday, Natalie bustles around the place like a wasp on steroids. She's clearly made a special effort for moving in day, getting the house as clean and welcoming as she's able to considering the state of the place. Flowers have been arranged on the table by the front door, and reed diffusers placed on shelves, as though making the farmhouse smell decent might detract from the chaos. What the house really could do with is a skip, and for every room to be emptied one by one: every archaic bit of furniture smashed to pieces; every remnant of the couple's life here to be thrown out along with the debris of Natalie's ancestry. I'd be the first in line to help.

Elsie is at nursery. If it wasn't for Natalie's nauseating fussing, the house would be quiet. It occurs to me how much nicer the place would be without her in it.

'Can I get you a cup of tea before you unpack your things, Kara? Just give us a shout if you need anything. I've got to pick up Elsie from nursery soon, but Jake and Tyler are both here if you need them.'

The noise of her fretting sets my nerves on edge. I wish she'd just shut up.

'I'll have a tea, if that's okay,' I say. 'I'll take the bags up while you're making it.'

Natalie heads to the kitchen. I take the suitcase up to the spare room. It's uninviting and soulless, a wasted space that could have so much potential. There's a double bed with a wooden frame, the floral bed linen matching the awful curtains. The carpet is faded and threadbare. The beautiful original fireplace that could be a focal point has been plaster-boarded over, only the mantelpiece still on show. There must be a tiled hearth beneath the carpet, but its beauty has presumably been hidden for years. Everything Natalie's parents did with the house seems to have been untouched, their daughter too afraid or too unwilling to make her own mark here. No wonder Jake feels trapped in a life that isn't his.

The thought of him moves me from the spare bedroom to his and Natalie's further along the landing. The door is ajar, so I push it open and stand on the threshold, an uninvited guest in their private space. The bed hasn't been made; the duvet is piled high at the end of the mattress and the sheet beneath dishevelled. I picture them here, seeing things I don't want to see. My face grows hot at the thought of them together, and a pounding of blood begins to fill my ears.

'Everything okay?'

I turn sharply at the sound of her voice behind me. I hadn't heard her on the stairs.

'It's lovely here,' I say. She smiles, but it isn't a fully committed gesture; there is something else behind her eyes. She's wondering what I'm doing here at the wrong bedroom door. She doesn't trust me. We've barely met and she knows nothing about me; but she has no reason to think anything more than she's seen. Is she having second thoughts, though? I'm going to have to work to keep this woman on side, but I'd already been prepared for that when I came here today.

'Your tea's ready when you are.'

I smile, and her response to me is immediately different; I see her face relax, the caution that was there just a moment ago now melted away. I wonder if she's really this easily reassured, or whether the change is a front to mask her suspicion. If it's a case of the former, my job here will be easy.

'I'll leave you to it.'

I go to the bathroom to pee. From the window, the patchwork of fields that stretches between here and the woodland that leads to the edge of the village can be seen. It's such a clear morning that the outlines of even the furthest hedgerows are in high definition, and a blaze of autumn colours gives a fire that manages to warm the air. It's beautiful here.

In the cupboard above the sink there's a pile of pill boxes: some over-the-counter sleeping tablets, the others antidepressants all prescribed to Natalie's name. Sertraline, Nytol, Melatonin. She must rattle when she jumps. I take a couple of the prescription boxes and turn them in my hand, wondering about the side effects of taking too many or too few after relying on them for so long. Jake rarely speaks about Natalie's dependence on medication, but he's told me enough for me to know just how reliant she is on it. It isn't difficult for anyone to see what a mess she is. She's a people pleaser, a relentless do-er: she tries to take on so much that she can't possibly fulfil anything to a good enough standard. In her attempts to be everything to everyone, her entire existence is haphazard. One of the many reasons her husband keeps coming back to me.

Thinking of Jake, I realise he's nowhere to be seen. He's probably hiding away in one of the barns. I move to put the boxes back in the cupboard, but I stop before I do so. A better idea comes to mind, one that might set in place a chain of events. It wouldn't be hard to make Natalie believe she's coming undone.

I empty the boxes of half their blister strips and pop the pills out in turn, with a plan to flush them down the toilet. Instead, I rip off a length of toilet paper and rest it on the cistern. I wrap up the pills and put them in my pocket, knowing they'll come in handy for later. Natalie will probably panic when she sees them gone and realises she doesn't have enough to see her through to her next prescription; she'll start to doubt herself, wondering whether there were really as many as she'd thought there were, how many she's really taken.

She needs these pills to function as a person: a wife, a business owner; a mother. What will become of her without them? And what would happen if she took too many, or if they fell into the wrong hands? The wrong mouth, even. Silly, careless Natalie. Whatever might she be capable of fucking up next?

SEVEN

On Wednesday, after collecting Elsie from nursery, Natalie takes her to Carmarthen to go clothes shopping. Despite still being small for her age, she had a growth spurt over the summer, her feet having gone up two shoe sizes between April and September, and now the weather's starting to grow colder she needs new things for winter. She arranged to meet with one of the mums from Elsie's nursery; there's rarely a chance to catch up with friends, and it'll be nice to stop for a bit of lunch or a coffee with the children.

They bypass the prettier side of the town, with the twelfth-century castle and the River Towy that runs past it, and head straight for the commercial part, with its web of shopping streets and generic retail brands. History and modernity sit in contrast alongside one another, though it occurs to Natalie that the high street could be in any UK town.

Her phone rings before they reach the first shop.

'We're not going to make it,' her friend tells her. 'I'm so sorry – Holly's just been sick in the back of the car.'

'Oh no. Is she okay?'

'It's just come from nowhere. I pulled over... I'm going to have to get her home.'

'Of course. I hope you're both okay. Let me know if I can do anything to help.'

'Will do. I'll text you later.'

Elsie is as disappointed as Natalie when she tells her Holly's been sick. It takes persuasion and a promise of ice cream to get Elsie into a clothes shop, and once in, she does little to cooperate.

'Elsie, please,' Natalie says, trying to wrangle her daughter's arm from a coat adorned with pink unicorns. 'It doesn't fit.'

The noise is instant. Elsie starts to wail like a siren, attracting looks of disapproval from other nearby shoppers.

'We'll find another one. Look, there's one with hearts on over there.'

The coat with the hearts doesn't come close to the one with the unicorns, and Elsie's crying ramps up a notch. When Natalie's phone starts ringing, she has to direct Elsie to the shop door with one hand, using the other to search her pocket.

It's an unknown number.

'Hello?'

'Hello, Mrs Prosser?'

'Yes.'

'I'm calling from St Paul's Hospital in Carmarthen,' the woman at the other end of the call tells her. 'It's about Elsie's heart check-up. Dr Aithal is currently unwell, I'm afraid, so we're going to have to cancel the appointment on Friday and we'll call you to reschedule when he's back at work.'

While the woman talks, Elsie throws herself onto the floor at the shop door, her face now an unnatural purple as she continues her screaming tantrum. Her doll's face-down in a puddle.

'Okay,' Natalie says, trying to peel Elsie off the floor while keeping the phone wedged between her shoulder and her ear. 'Thanks for letting me know.'

'We'll be in touch.'

Natalie shoves her phone back into her pocket and carries Elsie to a bench across the street, ignoring the stares of passing shoppers. 'Please, Elsie,' she begs her daughter as she sits her on her knee. 'Come on. Stop this, please.'

But Elsie won't be pacified.

'Would you like to go for that ice cream now?'

The screaming stops long enough for a snivelling Elsie to consider it. 'And Loulou?' she sniffs, gripping the doll with the now-muddied face.

Natalie exhales, relieved. 'And Loulou, of course. She told me she likes the chocolate fudge brownie best.'

Elsie pulls a face, unconvinced, bright enough to realise it'll be Natalie who eats the chocolate fudge brownie flavour. She allows Natalie to take her by the hand and they head towards a café where she knows they do nice ice cream sundaes. She visited a few times earlier in the year, stealing inspiration for her own shop. At the thought, she remembers the forthcoming pitch. Her heart flutters with excitement in a way it hasn't in a long time, and for what feels like the first time in forever, she allows herself to bask for a moment in the promise of expectation. Things may finally be looking up for them.

They are waiting at traffic lights, Natalie lost in a daydream, when she hears a familiar voice calling her name. She turns to see a friendly face approaching, May weaving between pedestrians as she tries to get her attention.

'Girls' shopping trip?' May asks.

Natalie pulls a face. 'That was the idea. Didn't quite go to plan.'

May crouches to Elsie. 'Gosh, you're getting a big girl. And how's Loulou doing? Still your best friend?'

Natalie has known May since she was a child, and she's

been the family's accountant for as long as Natalie is able to remember. She bought the doll as a Christmas present for Elsie nearly two years ago. Since then, they have been inseparable.

Elsie nods and pulls the doll to her chest.

'I'm glad she loves her so much,' May says, putting a hand on Natalie's arm as she straightens herself to stand. 'She's so adorable. And how are you, love?'

'I'm doing all right. We were just going to go for an ice cream, actually. Would you like to join us? They do a really good coffee.'

May hesitates. 'Why not? That would be lovely.'

'So how have you been?' Natalie asks, as they walk together.

'Oh, you know... bearing up.'

Natalie doesn't know what to say. May's ongoing health struggles are in many ways self-inflicted, though she manages somehow to keep going. She never says too much about it, so Natalie never likes to pry.

'How's everything at the farm?'

'Jake's pitching my ice cream to a supermarket next week. Fingers crossed.'

'I hope everything goes your way. You could do with some good luck, love.'

Natalie holds open the café door and ushers Elsie inside. They order sundaes and coffees, and while they chat, Natalie realises it's been a long time since she shared adult conversation beyond the farm. Even then, it's been restricted to talk of the cattle or money worries, and any discussion from Jake recently has been limited to what needs to be said. She misses conversation. She misses having a friend. The farm is so all-consuming it leaves little time for any social life and since Elsie was born it's been non-existent. Natalie misses having another woman to talk to.

'Elsie's doing all right then,' May says, watching as the little girl shoves a long-handled spoon into a sundae that's almost as long as her face.

'The doctors seem happy with her. She's been a bit tired, but that's probably part of the recovery.'

A few months ago, Elsie became unwell. It had started with tiredness, then a headache, then a rash. She was diagnosed with Kawasaki disease: something neither Natalie or Jake had heard of before. They were warned there might be possible long-term heart complications, so Elsie will need to see a specialist every six months until she's sixteen.

'Elsie,' Natalie says, when her daughter drops from her lap and kneels on the floor beneath the table. 'Come back up here, please. What's the matter?'

But before Elsie's able to respond, she vomits over the tiled floor of the café, a spray of squash and ice cream shooting over Natalie's and May's feet.

'Oh God, Elsie!' Natalie scoops her up in her arms. A second wave of nausea passes over her little grey face, and she is sick again, this time over Natalie's lap. The mother and son at the table next to them look on in disgust, but May is quick to react, grabbing a handful of napkins from the counter and asking a member of staff for a glass of water. Elsie is sobbing loudly, wailing in an incoherent babble that her tummy hurts. Natalie pulls her closer and cuddles her, but Elsie won't be consoled.

'Too much ice cream?' May asks, gently running a napkin under Elsie's chin, as a member of staff hurries over to clean up the mess.

'I don't know,' Natalie says, before apologising repeatedly to the poor woman handling the task of mopping up Elsie's regurgitated sundae from the floor. She turns to May and lowers her voice. 'Her little friend's been sick today too. There must be something going around at nursery. I should get her home.'

May helps Natalie and Elsie back to the car, and by the

time they get back to Llanafon, it's already getting dark. The farm looks beautifully eerie in the half-light, the decorations she put in place last week making the grounds look seasonally spooky.

She lifts Elsie out of her car seat and carries her to the house. As they approach the front door, Natalie notices something on the doorstep. She tries to hide it from Elsie for a moment, pointing out one of the ghosts in the trees that's got tangled in the wind, but Elsie isn't easily distracted and she spots the black form on the doorstep before Natalie is able to steer her around the side of the house.

'What's that?'

'It's nothing, sweetheart. Come on, let's get you inside.'

But Elsie's curiosity won't be diverted so easily. 'Dead, mummy,' she says, her voice barely a mumble. 'Dead.'

Natalie stares at the black outline on the doorstep, the dead crow's middle split open, its insides spilling across its bloodied wings. She feels watering in her cheeks: she has never dealt well with the sight of blood, and the crow looks bludgeoned, its injuries intentional.

'It's starting to rain,' she lies, taking Elsie by the arm. 'Let's get you inside.'

Before they reach the side door, Natalie senses movement near one of the barns. She stops and sees a flash of blue disappear into the barn. A blue much like that of one of the hoodies she's seen Kara wear. She wants to go and find out what she's doing there, but Elsie is heavy and limp in her arms. She needs to get her inside, in the warm.

Jake is in the kitchen, sitting at his laptop. He closes the lid when he sees them walk in, doing a double take when he sees the state of Natalie's clothes.

'Is everything okay? You're back late.'

'We saw May in town, we went for a coffee and some ice cream with her. Elsie's been sick,' she explains, gesturing to the stain on her jumper. 'I'm not sure whether she just ate too much, although Holly's been ill as well.'

She lowers Elsie onto one of the dining chairs and glances at the closed laptop, wondering what Jake didn't want her to see. This keeps happening recently, and it smarts that he must think her so naïve she hasn't noticed.

'Are you okay, sweetheart?' He runs a hand over Elsie's hair.

'Jake.' Natalie gestures to him to join her at the sink. Elsie has already slunk from the chair and gone to her wooden kitchen in the corner, but she lowers her voice anyway. 'There's a dead crow on the doorstep.'

He doesn't so much as bat an eyelid. 'I'll go and move it now.'

'Well, don't you think it's weird?'

'Not really. We live in the countryside.'

'But it's actually on the doorstep, like it's been placed there on purpose.'

'I'll move it now,' he says again, and, as she watches him head for the back door, she tries to ignore her frustration at his nonchalance. Sometimes, it's as though he doesn't feel anything anymore. What exactly would it take for him to react to something with some kind of emotion?

'Can you check the barns?'

'What for?'

'I thought I saw someone outside, just now.'

She sees him rolls his eyes before he leaves. But she knows what she saw just now. She knows she didn't imagine it.

She takes Elsie's new clothing from the bags and hangs each item over the back of one of the chairs to stop them getting creased. By the time Jake comes back in, she's started getting Elsie's dinner ready.

'Probably a fox,' he says, taking off his boots. 'I wouldn't worry about it; dead crows are a good omen, apparently.'

'Says who?'

'I don't know, I must have read it somewhere. Some people think they're a sign of good times to come.'

Not for the poor crow, she thinks. As far as she's aware, death has always been a symbol of disease or devastation. An ending, not a beginning. She doesn't see how the corpse of anything could be interpreted as positive, but she will have to take Jake's word for it.

'Did you go to the barns?'

'Yes,' he snaps. 'There's no one out there.'

When she goes upstairs later, she finds Kara lingering at their bedroom door. She's wearing what look like silk pyjamas, the type Natalie could never imagine herself wearing even if she could afford them. Her face is make-up free, and she still manages to look beautiful.

'Everything okay?'

'Oh. Sorry. I thought you'd already come upstairs.'

'Do you need anything?'

'Oh. Yes. Um... a hairdryer. Sorry. Mine's just broken. Do you have one I could borrow?'

Natalie sidesteps her to go into the bedroom. She goes around to her side of the bed and gets the hairdryer from the drawer of the dressing table.

'Thanks so much,' Kara says as she takes it from her. 'I'll bring it back to you when I'm done.'

What were you doing at the barns earlier? she wants to ask, but instead all she says is, 'No rush. I can get it back tomorrow.'

'Is Elsie okay now?'

'Yes, she's okay. Needs to sleep it off, I think.'

'Good. Goodnight then.'

Alone in bed a while later, Natalie looks up the meaning of dead crows online. Jake was right: apparently there are people who regard them as a symbol of positive things for the future.

Another detail catches Natalie's attention: that the appearance of a dead crow means the soul of someone who has passed is now at peace. The words catch her unprepared. It is meaningless, she tells herself. An old wives' tale.

When she switches the light off and turns over in bed, the exchange with Kara starts to play on her mind. Her hair wasn't wet when she spoke to her. Why did she need the hairdryer if she hadn't washed her hair? She hadn't heard it since she gave it to her either. So what was she doing hanging about outside her and Jake's bedroom door?

And then there's the other thing that keeps niggling at her with a persistence that won't be ignored. Kara had asked whether Elsie was okay now. But they hadn't seen Kara since arriving home from the shops. Kara had no way of knowing Elsie had been unwell.

EIGHT

The following morning, I take the keys to the ice cream shop from the top of the boiler and make my way around the darkened farmhouse. I carry the bag I prepared earlier, complete with Tupperware box, screwdriver and paintbrush; everything I need to set my plan in motion. When I get to the shop, I find it's not alarmed. Natalie must assume the farm's remote enough not to attract intruders, a complacency that invites trouble – she has enough experience to know there's no such thing as safe as houses.

In the darkness, I flash the torch on my phone across the room, not wanting to turn on the light. It's small but cosy in the shop, and Natalie's done her best to make the place warm and welcoming in a fashionably dated kind of way: mismatched armchairs that look as though they've been lifted from someone's grandparents' house, distressed wooden tables painted in various pastel shades; shabby chic dressers and soft furnishings. In one corner there's a box of children's toys; beside it, a narrow bookcase filled with board games and books. It's benefited from the kind of effort she's obviously never bothered to put into the house. She must care more for the comfort of her customers than she does for the comfort of her family.

I go to the freezer by the counter, where the display cases have been removed for winter and replaced with large tubs of labelled ice cream. Chocolate fudge brownie, pistachio, cookies and cream, salted caramel. I slide back the glass door and pull out the tub labelled salted caramel. I pull off the lid and dip a finger into the soft ice cream before licking it clean. It tastes delicious. Natalie really does make good ice cream.

I search the drawers for a spoon and take the tub of salted caramel with me to one of the armchairs, making myself as comfortable as it's possible to get in the cold before tucking in. Its sweetness sits on my tongue like melting candyfloss, and the taste reminds me of being a kid, transporting me back to a summer's evening and a fairground I'd forgotten all about: one of those travelling ones with rides that fold onto the back of lorries and never look safe enough to sit on.

The memory of that day arrives so suddenly that it sucks the breath from my lungs. I am there as though its sounds and colours can be caught from just outside the window. I can see myself, six or seven years old, one hand gripping a sugary cloud of candyfloss on a wooden stick, the other gripping my father's hand. My mother stands a few feet away from us, her silhouette illuminated by the flashing lights of the waltzers as she takes our photograph. She still has it somewhere, though I've not seen it for years. If only we'd known then, I think. I would have clutched his hand a little tighter. I would have never let it go.

Get a grip, I tell myself, and I shove the spoon back into the ice cream, shovelling another sickly mouthful between my teeth. I eat until I feel sick before returning the tub to the freezer, where I replace the lid. Then I wash the spoon and return it to the drawer, leaving everything as I found it. In the darkness, I stand with my lower back pressed against the edge of the sink and try to smother the urge to trash the shop. I picture myself pulling the framed artwork from the walls, ripping open cushions; smashing equipment with my bare hands. And for a moment, imagining it makes me feel better. Just before I'm brought crashing back to the claustrophobic silence of the present, and the unfairness of it all. I imagine Jake stirring in bed, an arm reaching over Natalie's body beneath the warmth of the duvet. For a moment, in his still half-asleep state, he thinks it's me beside him. He sees us as we were the last time we were able to share a bed together, my body beneath his under the duvet. His hands roam and his mind wakens, and just as I am now, he is jolted to reality. I imagine the rush of disappointment, taking comfort in it. I wonder how often he thinks of me when he's with her.

Rage rushes through me. Sometimes, in my worst moments, it feels like a separate part of myself: a living thing over which I have no control. And yet I do; I wouldn't be able to be here if I didn't. Feel one thing and behave as another – it is a mantra that's become a part of who I am. So I take a deep breath and let the anger burn through me until it fizzles out and fades away. I remind myself why I came here. Time is against me now, so I take the screwdriver from my pocket and go to the back of the freezer. I find its cable, feeling my way along until I locate the plug at the wall. I unscrew it and remove the fuse, replacing it with the dead one in my pocket. I put the plug back in and make sure the switch at the wall is still turned on, then I check that everything else is as I found it when I came in.

By the time Natalie comes in here next, all her hard work will be undone and there'll be nothing for Jake to take to the pitch. She will blame herself, wondering what she did wrong; questioning herself over every detail of the last time she was in here. Little by little, I will prove this woman can't be trusted with anything. Natalie is too careless. She leaves things lying around in places where anyone might get their hands on them. Medication boxes. Keys. Letters from the hospital.

I take the bag outside with me and lock up, then I take out the Tupperware box and the paintbrush. The night air will dry my graffiti quickly enough, so that by the time Natalie finds my message, the letters will have stained the glass. I finish my task and stand back to admire my efforts. A single word, recriminatory. I allow myself to bask for a moment in the possibilities of her reaction; her questions over the whos and the whys. Let her wonder, just as I have, whether everything is really as it seems.

NINE

With Elsie still in bed sleeping off yesterday's sickness, and Tyler and Jake having left early that morning to pick up a new piece of machinery for the milking barn, Natalie sets about making the cakes she promised she'd bake for the nursery's fundraising event tomorrow morning. She'd planned to take them there before going to the hospital for Elsie's appointment, but now it's been cancelled, and Elsie will need forty-eight hours at home, she'll ask Jake to take them for her. She puts the kettle on and gets the baking equipment and ingredients from the cupboards. She mixes a simple batter and scoops it into cupcake holders, then once they're in the oven she calls Holly's mum.

'How's she doing this morning?' she asks.

'Fine. Like nothing happened. How about Elsie?' Natalie had texted her the night before to say Elsie had also been sick.

'Still sleeping.'

'I hope she's all right when she wakes up. Let me know later how she's doing.'

When the call's ended, Natalie gets a packet of mince from

the fridge and an onion from the vegetable rack; if she makes dinner now it'll save her time later when Elsie's awake. She's frying the onion when Kara appears in the doorway, perfect, making Natalie feel self-conscious. Her make-up is expertly applied, her hair styled in beach waves as though she's just come from a salon, and even in jeans and a T-shirt she manages somehow to look as though she's ready for a night out.

'The kettle's not long boiled. Would you like one?'

She can't shake the thought that it was Kara she saw out by the barns the previous evening, but she doesn't want to seem suspicious around her. They've never told her not to go beyond the house, and she supposes Kara has every right to explore the farm.

But why would she have tried to hide herself from Natalie's view?

'You read my mind. A coffee would be great, thanks.'

Natalie reaches for the kettle. 'Did I see you out by the barns yesterday evening?'

Kara pulls a face. 'Yes. I went for a run, got lost in the lanes and somehow ended up coming back through the fields. I'm so sorry. I saw you and Elsie and I didn't want you to think I'd been snooping around. Sorry, it was stupid, really.'

Natalie smiles, alleviating Kara's awkwardness. It would make sense that a stranger to the area would get lost, especially with it now getting dark so early.

'I'm making spag bol for tonight – it's Elsie's favourite. Hopefully she'll be able to eat some. Would you like to join us for dinner?'

Natalie has wondered what Kara actually eats, assuming it to be very little. She hasn't seen her consume anything more than tea, coffee and fruit since she moved in, though perhaps Kara has used the kitchen while everyone else has been out. If so, she's been very tidy.

'Oh, I wouldn't like to intrude.'

'You wouldn't be at all. It'll just be me and Elsie – Jake's going for a pint with Tyler tonight.'

'Well, only if you're sure, that would be lovely, thanks.' She gestures to the saucepan on the hob. 'Can I do anything to help?'

'It's all done. Thanks though. You could do me a favour, if you don't mind. Stir that for me while I use the bathroom.'

Natalie goes to use the toilet, and when she comes back downstairs, Kara is pulling a tray of burned cupcakes from the oven.

'Shit. I'd forgotten they were in there.'

'I reckon they can be salvaged,' Kara assures her.

'Really?' Natalie assesses the crisp brown edge of one of the cakes, unconvinced.

'It's all in the presentation. You can hide anything if you make it look pretty enough. Here.' She reaches for a knife from the block on the worktop. 'Have you made the icing yet?'

She raises an eyebrow. 'Do I look that organised to you?'

Kara smiles. 'You sort the mince, and I'll sort out these. If that's okay with you?'

'Of course,' Natalie says. 'Thank you.' She passes Kara the butter and the sugar, along with the ready-made fondant icing she'd bought with the ambitious hope of making some decorative flowers.

'You said you work in IT,' she says, as she stirs the bolognese. She's wanted to know more about Kara's job since they first met, intrigued by how the other woman spends her days. 'How did that come about?'

'Accidentally really. It was never the plan. I was studying law at university, but I had to give it up when my father became ill.'

'What was wrong with him?' Natalie bites her lip. 'I'm sorry, I shouldn't have asked that. You don't have to tell me.'

Kara turns a cupcake onto its side and slices off the burnt

top. 'It's fine. It's nice to talk to someone about him. He had dementia. It was a very progressive and debilitating form. He couldn't look after himself for the last couple of years. I quit to look after him.'

'That's a big responsibility. You were a good daughter to him.'

'I don't know about that. I'll always wish there was something more I could have done. After he died, I figured the best thing I could do for him now is live my life the way I want it. He'd want me to take every opportunity. That's why I'm here.'

Natalie feels a sudden swell of sadness rise in her chest, the thought of her own parents catching her off-guard. She is grateful when the noise of the electric whisk cuts short their conversation.

They work in silence for a while, Natalie preparing dinner for later while Kara deals with the icing. Her earlier suspicions of Kara now feel embarrassingly misplaced.

'Oh wow,' Natalie says, admiring the sugar paste rose Kara's handcrafted seemingly without effort. 'That's beautiful.'

'I'll pipe the buttercream for you once the cakes have cooled. Will they do?'

'Perfect. They'll be too good to eat. Thank you so much.'

'Next time,' Kara says with a smile, crafting another rose with dextrous fingers, 'order some from Tesco.'

Natalie laughs. 'Good plan.' This is nice, she thinks. It feels so normal and welcome; everything she'd been hoping for. So far, Kara's been the perfect guest. Then Natalie remembers her at her bedroom door. The way she'd asked after Elsie when she had no reason to know she'd been unwell.

'Kara. Last night, when you asked after Elsie, how did you know she'd been sick?'

'Jake told me.'

Natalie says nothing, but something doesn't seem to add up.

Jake had been downstairs when they'd got home. He'd gone outside to deal with the dead crow on the doorstep, and after he came back in she can't remember him going upstairs. As far as Natalie can make out, they didn't have a chance to see one another. But she must have got it wrong, she tells herself. She's got confused somewhere.

How could she confuse something like that, though? She'd either seen Jake or she hadn't.

'Oh shit.'

'What's the matter?'

'I haven't fed the animals.' Jake usually does it, but as he'd needed to leave so early that morning Natalie had told him she'd see to it. With Elsie ill and the cakes to make, she'd forgotten all about it.

'Go and do to it now,' Kara says. 'I can finish up here.'

'Are you sure? Thank you so much.'

Natalie goes to the cattle first and puts out the feed, apologising to the cows aloud for her lateness as she sets about the task. The cow who was unwell the week before seems to have made a turnaround, the antibiotics finally having taken effect. Once she's finished in the barn, she goes to the pigsty. Peppa and George are both stretched out on the mud, though Peppa's interest is stirred by the arrival of breakfast. As Natalie feeds them, her thoughts stray to Jake's forthcoming pitch with Adler's. Perhaps she should get a second opinion on her latest batch of ice cream: Jake and Tyler are both biased; she doubts either of them would tell her if it wasn't to usual standards. Maybe she'll ask Kara. It would be good to get someone else's feedback.

She finishes feeding the pigs and heads for the ice cream shop at the other side of the farmhouse. She senses something wrong before she gets there, her gut instinctively warning her that all is not right. When she turns the corner, she sees the paint scrawled across the window, the printed red letters covering the glass in an angry accusation. *SCUM*.

She feels bile rise in her mouth.

'Natalie!' She turns at the sound of Kara's voice. She is wearing Jake's wellies. 'What's happened? Are you okay?'

And then Natalie sees Elsie standing just behind her, having come downstairs while Natalie was outside and followed Kara from the house. 'Can you take her inside?' she urges her. 'I don't really want her to see this.'

Kara's eyes drift to the graffitied shop window. She does as requested, taking Elsie by the hand and leading her back to the house. Natalie finds herself unable to pull her eyes from the word. There's a part of her that expected this at some point. But she hadn't realised it would punch her in the gut as painfully as this.

She doesn't know how long she's been there when she hears Jake's van pull onto the driveway.

'Natalie. Natalie!'

Natalie hears his footsteps on the gravel, sees him stop short when he sees the graffitied window.

'Jesus.' He comes to her and places a hand on her back.

'I didn't notice anything this morning,' he explains. 'It was still dark when I left.'

'Why would someone do this?' she manages to speak at last.

Jake turns her to him. She allows him to hold her for a moment before working herself free of the embrace to glance over his shoulder, the feeling they're being watched too strong to ignore. Kara is standing at the side of the house, still wearing Jake's wellies; a hand on Elsie's shoulder as she gazes at them.

Natalie turns away and goes to the window, putting a hand to the glass despite Jake's protests. 'Natalie, don't. Let me deal with it.'

Ignoring him, she puts a hand to the smear of red that forms the bottom curve of the letter C. She presses her fingertips against the colour, rubbing them so that it transfers onto her skin. Then she puts her fingertips to her nose.

Bile returns, thicker, more acidic now. 'It isn't paint,' she tells him. 'It's blood.'

TEN

I finish getting ready in the bathroom upstairs before going down to see Jake and Natalie. I want to make a point of seeing them before I leave the farm. Or rather, I want to make a point of them seeing me. They're in the kitchen; I hear the tapping of Jake's laptop and dishes being stacked on the draining board as Natalie does the washing-up. The atmosphere on the farm has been tense since yesterday's attack on the shop, and I've done my best to stay out of the way where possible.

When I hear the murmur of conversation, I stop in the hallway to listen.

'I don't care what the police said,' I hear Natalie saying, 'it doesn't make any sense.'

'I'm reading about it here,' Jake replies. 'A few farms in Pembrokeshire have been targeted by protesters. We already talked about preparing ourselves for possible backlash.'

I hear Natalie sigh. 'No vegan's going to make a stand against so-called animal cruelty by using blood to make their point. And we don't even know what that blood's come from.' Her voice cracks. She's close to tears. 'It doesn't make sense.'

'They told us they'll look into it, so I suppose we've just got to wait and see.'

'Did you tell them about the bloody handprint you found on the gate?'

'Yes. Whoever's responsible must have left it by mistake on their way out.'

'They're not in any rush to come to take fingerprints though,' she says bitterly. She clangs something on the draining board. 'And what about the ice cream? It's all ruined – I can't get more made in time for the pitch.'

'I'll speak to Adler's,' Jake tries to reassure her. 'I'll tell them there's been a family emergency, that we need to rearrange the date.'

Something smashes to the floor, and I hear Natalie swear beneath her breath. 'How did it happen though? It's too much of a coincidence.'

'No one got into the shop,' Jake tells her, with a voice that suggests they've already had this conversation. 'It's just unfortunate timing, that's all.'

'So how did it happen?' she says again. 'All the plugs were switched on.'

'I don't know,' Jake snaps.

They fall into silence. I wonder if this is how things usually are, regardless of recent events; if every evening is passed in the silence of the ambivalence they seem to have both accepted.

I break the silence when I move to the doorway, resting a hip against the doorframe and posing as though for a photographer. Natalie is crouched at the floor with a dustpan and brush, sweeping up pieces of broken glass.

'Ooh,' she says when she sees me, her voice altered, adopting a forced cheeriness. 'Look at you all dressed up. Off anywhere nice?'

'Maybe,' I say, catching Jake's eye. 'Who knows where the night may end.'

I see Natalie eye me with curiosity. She's right about what I know she's thinking: there's nowhere to go out around here. But I'm not going out around here. I made a point to arrange this evening somewhere far from home, somewhere no one from around here will see me. I just need Jake to know that I'm going somewhere. I need him to wonder at the possibilities of what I might have planned.

'I'm meeting up with an old friend,' I say, knowing Natalie's curiosity won't be satisfied by my previous answer. 'She's visiting Aberystwyth with work, so I thought it made sense to catch up while she's in this part of the country.'

'Well, have a good evening,' Natalie says. 'Don't do anything I wouldn't.'

I laugh. Jake hasn't taken his eyes off me. His face tells me everything I need to know. He hates this. He's jealous and wants to question me about where I'm going and who I'm really going with, but he can't because his wife's in the room. And who is he to question me, when he's the one who's been living two lives, the bigger liar of the two of us?

I get in the car and drive for an hour, heading for Aberystwyth. We've arranged to meet in a hotel just outside the town centre, everything booked under his name. I'm not an idiot; I know the dangers, but I've triple-checked everything and I'm satisfied he's not some internet nutter. Besides, I can look after myself.

I only know the man's name because it appeared as part of his profile, an obligatory introduction that had we met in some other way beyond the realms of the internet I might not have bothered to find out. I know what I need to – what he looks like and where we're meeting. Everything else is surplus detail.

It's been so long since I had sex with someone who isn't Jake that I've forgotten what it's like with another man. I feel an excitement I know I shouldn't. This is how it felt with Jake and me at the start – dangerous and unpredictable. Now, I'm getting bored of waiting for him. He needs to realise I can't do this forever. I want him to experience the kind of jealously I have to live with every day.

By the time I get to the hotel – a generic, budget chain with a building that resembles university halls – his car's already there. He'd given me a description of it, and when I pull in, I see it near the front entrance. I hope he looks like he does in his pictures. The last thing I need is to be catfished. Of course, he's also seen photographs of me. He liked what he saw, and when I get out of the car he clearly recognises me straight away.

He's older than I am, maybe late-thirties, well-groomed and attractive in the predictable, safe way that city men tend to be. He's not my usual type, whatever my usual type is. It occurs to me I don't even have one. Jake. But this man is nothing like him. He's clean-shaven and dressed in a suit, an office type who probably wouldn't know one end of a piece of machinery from another; the kind of man who pays other men for anything involving manual labour. I see him look me up and down as he gets out from the car, assessing me as though he's about to make a purchase, so I do the same, wondering whether he'll appreciate the appraisal.

'Ashley,' he says, greeting me with the false name I gave him – I obviously don't want him to know my real one. The first thing he's likely to have done is try to find me online.

'Hi.' I nod towards the hotel entrance. 'How do you want to play this?'

My choice of words makes him smile. 'I'll check in and then I'll send you a room number; what do you think?'

'Fine by me.'

He goes to the boot of the car and pulls out an overnight bag and a rucksack. I hear a clink of bottles as he pulls out the latter. He'll be disappointed if he thinks I'm going to join him for a drink; staying overnight here would be a step too far.

'See you soon,' he says.

I go back to my car and get out my phone, waiting for him to contact me via the website through which we've been talking for the past week or so. I'm just starting to think I've been stood up in the most embarrassing of ways when I finally get a message from him, letting me know he's in room 109. I sit in the car a few minutes longer before heading into the hotel and walking past the reception to the staircase. When I get to the first floor, I find room 109; he's there with a glass in his hand.

'Thanks,' I say, taking it with no intention of drinking any. I'm not an idiot. I've spiked drinks, so I know just how easy it can be to fool someone into a false sense of security.

'I need to use the bathroom first.' I put my drink next to the phone. While I'm in the bathroom, I hear him lock the bedroom door. I use the toilet before checking my reflection in the mirror. When I go back out, he's sitting on the bed waiting for me. My glass is still by the phone; his is in his hand.

'We don't need to waste time with that,' I tell him, and I take it from him, placing it next to mine. He smiles at my insistence before I straddle him on the bed and start to undo his shirt. His hands explore my stomach before moving down and grappling with my clothes, and then he sits up and pulls me towards him, forcing his tongue in my mouth. He grips the hair at the back of my head as he kisses me, and when I try to catch my breath, his grasp doesn't give up.

'Easy,' I warn him, but at the same time I push back and start to unzip his trousers. He wriggles free of them before sitting upright to watch me undress. He gets up from the bed, his eyes fixed on me, and then he puts his hands on my shoulders and pushes me to my knees.

I have always had a high sex drive. Insatiable, that's the word Jake once used to describe me. Now, I close my eyes and picture Jake's strong body in front of mine. When this stranger pulls me up from the carpet and turns me to bend me over the bed, it's Jake's weight I feel press down upon my back: Jake's hands that hold me in place. I open my eyes, relax into it while I'm able to distract myself with thoughts of Jake, images of his body transporting me. And then guilt washes over me. There's a part of me that hates myself for what I'm doing. But it's not my fault, I tell myself: it's his. If only Jake had left her when he'd first said he was going to, I wouldn't be here. I wouldn't be doing this. I wouldn't need to be doing any of the things I'm doing. He's responsible for all of it.

The man finishes and pulls away from me before collapsing on the bed with a sigh. I get up and reach for a glass, making sure it's the one that was closest to the phone: the one he had given me earlier.

'Here we go,' I say, handing it to him. 'You've earned that.'

He shuffles across the bed to make room for me to prop myself on the next pillow. I wait for him to take a sip, knowing that if he's spiked it with something I'll soon find out. I don't suspect he has; it's just my overactive imagination running into fiction. When you're as guilty as I am you tend to grow suspicious of everyone.

I get out my phone and check it to see whether Jake's got in touch. I'm half expecting a message asking where I've really gone or who I'm really with, but there's nothing. Either Natalie has been around him all evening and he's been unable to text or he's leaving me to sweat, and I'm guessing it's the latter. Either way, he needs to find out about tonight. There's no way I can just tell him – that would spoil the effect entirely. I can't tell him yet. He needs to suffer first, the way I have. The not knowing. The wondering what-if.

But if tonight has served no other purpose, it's confirmed a truth I've always known: that it's Jake and only Jake. I glance at the man beside me, repulsed now by his nakedness. I want to go home. I want to go back to Jake and make him mine, for good this time, no matter what it takes.

ELEVEN

Friday afternoon sees a spell of dry weather, so Natalie allows Elsie to roam in the outdoor play area by the ice cream shop while she scrubs the blood from its windows. It's surprisingly stubborn, staining the glass with a pink smear, and with every burst of energy she feels nausea rise in her chest, the smell that refuses to subside catching in her throat. She doesn't want to contemplate where the blood might have come from.

She's offered a welcome break from her thoughts when her phone starts ringing: an unknown number. It's the hospital.

'Elsie didn't attend her check-up with Dr Aithal this morning,' the woman says. 'Is everything okay?'

Natalie's stomach twists. 'I had a call from you,' she says. 'On Wednesday. I mean, not from you, but from someone at the hospital.'

'What call was this?'

'A call to say the appointment was being cancelled because Dr Aithal's unwell.' There is silence at the other end of the line. 'Hello?'

'Did the person who called you give you their name?'

Natalie realises that a name had never been offered; it

didn't occur to her to ask for one. Elsie had been having a melt-down when she'd taken the call, and amid all the chaos, Natalie hadn't been thinking straight.

'Is there something wrong?' she asks, panic setting in.

'Dr Aithal has been at work all week. No calls have been made from this department to cancel any of his appointments.'

'That can't be right. I got a phone call.'

'I'm sorry, Mrs Prosser. I can assure you that call didn't come from anyone in our department. Shall we rearrange? I'm afraid Dr Aithal doesn't have any free appointments now until the week after next.'

'That'll be fine,' Natalie tells her, and after the call's ended she makes a note of the new appointment day and time on her phone. The crow, the shop, now this. It isn't a coincidence, and she won't have Jake try to make her believe otherwise. She can't tell him about this. He'll blame her for not checking who the caller was, for not making sure it was really the hospital. But why would she have thought anything different?

She continues to scrub the windows, but when she looks over her shoulder to check on Elsie, her daughter is on the ground.

'Elsie!'

She didn't hear her fall or cry out, and when Natalie gets to Elsie, the little girl looks as though she's about to fall asleep. 'Are you okay, sweetheart?'

'Tired,' Elsie manages to speak.

Natalie carries her into the house and puts her into bed. Elsie feels cold, her fingers icy. This can't be a sickness bug. Holly is already better, so why isn't Elsie? She gets out her phone and calls the surgery, the receptionist telling her they'll see her within the hour if she can get her there. They know Elsie's medical history; they're not going to take any chances.

Elsie sleeps in the car on the way to the surgery. The doctor checks her over and after hearing about Elsie's lethargy and sickness she advises a blood test, just to be on the safe side. Elsie cries when the blood is taken, so Natalie promises her a film and a treat when they get home. She'll be with Jake tonight as Natalie has a shift at the pub, though she's sure he won't object to the suggestion.

Before leaving the house for the pub, Natalie checks the call log on her phone. She knows exactly when she received the call from the hospital, or whoever it was; it's easy to remember thanks to Elsie's meltdown in Carmarthen. But when she scrolls back through the incoming and outgoing calls, it isn't there. There's no record of an answered call from an unknown number.

After walking home from the pub at gone 10 p.m., Natalie's cold to her bones, exhausted from overthinking. She lets herself in through the side door, leaving her shoes in the porchway; when she goes into the kitchen, she rolls her eyes at the dirty plates in the sink. Jake could have dealt with them after he put Elsie to bed, but then she's distracted by the corkscrew left on the dining table. Jake rarely drinks, and never alone. Unless, she thinks, he's not alone.

She treads carefully through the kitchen and into the hallway. The living room door's ajar, and through the gap she can see the glow of a lit fire. It seems to offer the only source of light; the rest of the room's shrouded in the darkness of night. It looks romantic, like the kind of evening they've not shared together in years, since before Elsie was born. *Stop it*, she tells herself. *You're being paranoid.* She pauses at the living room door. Jake is sitting at the end of the sofa, his back to her. His hair has been washed – she can always tell by the softness of it, as yet untouched by the harshness of the elements. She hears Kara's voice before she sees her: the high, lilted tinkle of her laugh, like a spoon tapped against a glass. What the hell is there for them to be laughing at?

'That was so funny,' she hears Kara say. 'She's so cute.'

Natalie edges quietly to the doorway and sees Kara sitting on the sofa alongside Jake, just a couple of feet away from him. Her red hair is swept to the side, resting on one shoulder, and she's wearing a dressing gown. It's hanging loose at her chest, her collarbones exposed. There's an open bottle of red wine and two glasses on the table.

'I don't know where it came from,' Jake says. 'You wonder where they pick this stuff up.'

Natalie feels a burning sensation in her chest. Whatever Elsie has said or done, she wasn't there to witness it. They're sharing a memory she wasn't a part of, and it makes her feel like an outsider in her own home.

'Evening.'

Jake turns at her voice. 'You're back early,' he says, and the words make him sound guilty, as if she's walked in on something he hadn't planned for her to see.

'Quiet night,' she lies. The pub was busy, and she made too many mistakes, her mind distracted by Elsie's health and thoughts of the attack on the shop. The landlord told her she could leave early. She has a raging headache and feels sick with tiredness, but she doesn't want to tell Jake any of this, especially not with Kara there.

'You look tired.'

Natalie can't quite interpret his tone. There's no sympathy or concern in it; he's delivering a point of fact, in the way someone might comment on the rain starting.

'I'm fine.'

She notices Kara pull her dressing gown tighter across her chest.

'I found out what happened to the freezer in the shop,' Jake tells her. 'I took the plug apart. The fuse was dead.'

'We've had it less than a couple of years. It shouldn't have gone already. Is it still under warranty?'

'I contacted the company earlier. I'll call again on Monday if they've not got back to me by then.' He sees her eyeing the bottle of wine and there's an awkward moment of silence that stretches for longer than is comfortable. 'Do you want a glass?'

She shakes her head. She has work at the pub again for the next two days over the weekend, and on Monday she'll have to make more ice cream in time for Jake to be able to pitch it. How can he sit here smiling and laughing after what happened yesterday? And when she tries to remember the last time he laughed with her, Natalie can't recall it.

She notices now for the first time that Kara hasn't spoken since she came home; to Natalie her silence feels like guilt. She doesn't want to think what she's thinking, but the idea of it has taken hold of her and is refusing to let go.

She wants to ask what they were laughing about just now, what it was that Elsie has said to amuse them, but doing so would mean admitting she was listening in on their conversation. If she does that, they'll both know she's suspicious. And of what? They weren't doing anything.

She's being silly, she tells herself. Kara's only doing tonight with Jake what she did with her just a couple of days ago: sharing a drink and conversation. They're simply getting to know one another better. He's making an effort – she can hardly complain now that he's doing the very thing she'd asked of him.

'I'm going to bed.'

'Me too,' Kara says.

'Goodnight.'

Natalie leaves them to it and heads upstairs to check on Elsie. By the time she's brushed her teeth and gone to her own bedroom, she's heard Kara go to hers. Minutes later, Jake joins Natalie. She watches him as he undresses, and when he gets into bed he comments on how cold it is. She moves closer to him, but he turns his back to her. The rejection stings. A small snake of doubt has been working its way into her for a while; now, it sits heavy in her chest, refusing to be ignored. Jake doesn't want her any more. She only hopes it isn't because he's found someone else.

TWELVE

After Natalie leaves for work the following afternoon, Jake tells me he's going to finish cleaning the milking equipment. He asks me if I'd mind keeping an eye on Elsie, which of course I'm happy to – she's mostly quiet and keeps herself to herself, happy to amuse herself with her toys. When she eventually tires of making me imaginary cups of tea and plates of food with plastic vegetables, I take her into the living room and put on the television, keeping her glued to the sofa for five minutes with a tray of snacks.

When I go back into the kitchen, Jake is at the sink washing his hands. I run my hands through his hair. He flinches from my touch, too cautious to respond with his own, yet he doesn't move away. He allows me to kiss him before turning his face away.

'We can't,' he mutters.

'We can.'

I put a hand under his shirt, my fingers tracing the hard contours of his stomach. He closes his eyes for a moment before grabbing my arm and pushing it away.

'This isn't working.'

'What isn't working?'

'This,' he says, moving away from me. 'You being here.'

I'm about to unleash a tirade when we hear Elsie calling from the living room. 'I'll go,' I tell him. 'You do what you need to.'

He turns back before he gets to the door, as though he's no longer sure about leaving Elsie with me.

'We'll be fine,' I reassure him. 'All of us.'

After Jake heads out, I go to Elsie, who tells me she doesn't want to watch TV. I ask her what she'd like to do, and when she says play with her doll's house I follow her upstairs to her bedroom. I watch her line three generations of tiny doll family outside their house while she talks to them in riddles only she understands – something about a teacher and a mermaid and a worm. While she's entertained, I go further along the landing and into Jake and Natalie's bedroom, pushing the door closed behind me.

It feels strange to be in their room, and yet it doesn't feel wrong. If anything, it feels a kind of strangeness that over time might become commonplace. I belong to this place. I deserve to be here. I sit on the bed and run my hands over the faded floral duvet cover. It's not what I would choose for the place. Their bedroom's the same as the rest of the house: a shrine to the past. Natalie and Jake have had years to bring this place to some form of glory, yet they appear to have done little since her parents died, allowing it to remain a living museum to the 1990s.

No wonder Jake feels trapped here. He has been ensnared in Natalie's world, a world she's also too scared to walk away from, her entire adult life forged by her parents' passing. There were conversations, presumably. Jake and Natalie must have talked of alternative lives somewhere during all their years together, but at some point those dreams and possibilities of a different future were cast aside in place of the familiar and the safe. And now everything is stale, a fact his coming to me confirms. He has talked to me about his life here with her. I wonder if he's discussed it with me more than he ever has with Natalie.

My reflection stares back at me from the mirror of the wardrobe door. Sometimes, when I look at myself, I don't recognise the person who looks back at me. I still expect to see a teenager, fresh-faced and full of enthusiasm, but time and experience have hardened me. I wonder whether Jake thinks the same when he looks at me. I saw the way he looked at me yesterday. He still wants me, maybe more now than he ever has. It's been too long since we last had sex. The pressure of the three of us here together might be starting to get to him, but I don't know if it's that alone. Sometimes, I've worried recently he's having doubts about us. About me.

I pull my gaze from my reflection and look around the room, wondering whether Natalie's parents stared at this same scene all those years ago: the drab beige walls, the floral-patterned curtains; the old-fashioned faux-oak wardrobe, the kind that takes up a quarter of a room yet manages not to store much. It's like a looming, stony-faced guardsman, watching over me as though it knows what I'm guilty of. Its doors don't close properly; in front of them, one of Elsie's soft toys – an oversized owl with glittering pink wings – is used to prop them shut. I kick it aside. The heavy doors swing open with a tired creak, exposing the clothing crammed onto the rail and shoved in haphazard piles on the floor. It is easy to see where Natalie's things end and Jake's begin, a clear divide between rainbow colours and every shade of greys and blues. I run my hand over the fabrics, my fingertips caressing hard denims and worn cottons, coarse wools and weather-proof polyester. There are no silks here – no satins or linens. Life on the farm requires practical, hard-wearing attire, and Jake and Natalie have nothing that remotely resembles a social life beyond their five hundred acres of this land.

I recall the last night Jake and I spent together, so long ago now it feels more like years than months. We met up in Swansea, far enough away that no one he knew would see him there, and we spent the evening eating and drinking in a restaurant neither of us could really afford. He insisted on footing the bill, I suspect as much through guilt as generosity – he'd already been saying for too long that he was going to leave Natalie. I forgave him for the fact it still hadn't happened, like I always have, because I wanted him so badly.

We went back to a hotel and had sex that lasted into the early hours of the morning. I'd never seen Jake as he was that night, unincumbered and more adventurous than he'd ever been. We laughed and drank and explored each other's bodies like a couple of teenagers on the brink of some kind of sexual awakening, free for those few blissful hours from responsibility and burden. For the first time in a long time, he was him, the Jake he was always supposed to be. And for the first time in even longer, I could be just me.

'What are you doing?'

Elsie's voice breaks me from my daydream. She stands in the doorway holding a half-eaten apple in one hand and a tube of toothpaste in the other, her curly hair matted and stuck to the sides of her face.

'What are you doing?' I ask back, noticing that the lid of the toothpaste is missing and realising now why Elsie's hair's been stuck to her skin. I go to her and put a hand on her curls, which are thick with sticky globs of blue and red. 'Elsie,' I sigh. 'Toothpaste is for teeth. There's a clue in the name.'

She grins at me before racing back down the corridor to the bathroom. I should probably follow her to assess the damage she's managed to create in the minutes my attention has been distracted in this room, or intervene before further chaos ensues, but I don't, instead sitting back on the bed and returning to my memories of Jake's naked body in that hotel bed.

The other man appears, an intrusive thought that takes me

back to that hotel room: his body in front of me; his weight pressing down on my back. I sit up and shake myself from the memory, my chest burning with regret. But the shame only brings back all the bad things, a flood that gathers and washes over me. Sometimes bad deeds are needed. A necessary evil.

I get up and go to Elsie's room. She's dressed herself in a bright-pink tutu and plastic high-heel dressing-up shoes that she's wearing on the wrong feet. She turns and sees me in the doorway before twirling like a ballerina, putting on a performance for her audience. She's part of the package, I realise that. If I'm to get Jake, his daughter will have to come too. But it's not simply a case of whether I'm prepared to accept her; it's as much about whether she's prepared to accept me. But young children are malleable. Impressionable. A seed of doubt planted about her mother's capabilities – a few words to suggest that looking after Elsie might not be what Natalie wants. That's the other thing about children – they never forget. Their minds may be small, yet to develop, but they retain information and memory with a capacity that far exceeds most people's expectation. Natalie will never leave her daughter but perhaps, with a few choice words and enough repetition, Elsie will distance herself from her mother. When it comes to the courts, a bright and self-assured child, even one as young as Elsie, must be granted some choice in where she spends her future?

Tired of delivering her solo performance, Elsie flops back onto the carpet and begins to play with her dolls, paying me no further attention. She looks so content, so happy here, that I realise it would be a kind of cruelty to rip her from the only home she's ever known and to thrust her into a new life without warning. She belongs here, where she knows she's safe. Jake wants to leave this place – he has always wanted to leave this place, but perhaps that's not really what's right for him. Perhaps that's not what's right for *us*. I love it here. It's Elsie's home. She belongs to this farm as much as her father does. They belong here as much as I do.

I return to Jake and Natalie's bedroom, close the door behind me. I lie back on the bed and prop myself against the pillows, my mind transporting me to an imagined future weekend: Sunday morning, Elsie still asleep in her room; a block of early morning sunshine pushing through the gaps in the curtains and settling upon the curve of Jake's body beneath the duvet. Me, beside him, in my rightful place.

I smooth the duvet at my sides and lie back on the bed, closing my eyes and allowing myself to get lost in my daydream. For the first time in a long time, the anger melts from me as though it's never existed. It feels lighter in my head, my brain in these moments a much easier place for my consciousness to be in. We could be happy here. This could really be it. Finally, I feel as though I'm home.

THIRTEEN

By the time Monday arrives, Natalie is exhausted. The pub was busy on both Saturday and Sunday nights, and she finished late both evenings. Thoughts of Jake and Kara alone in the house taunted her throughout her shifts, though both evenings when she arrived home they weren't together. Maybe being caught on Friday evening was a warning to them to be more careful. Or perhaps, she tries to tell herself, it was nothing. Kara's alone here, with no friends locally. Jake was being friendly. But the bottle of wine is unusual; Jake rarely drinks wine.

And how friendly is too friendly?

On Monday, Natalie prepares everything she needs to make more ice cream. She calls the nursery early to ask if she can pay for Elsie to stay with them a full day rather than a half, something she's never done before. She feels guilty – she will only see her daughter for a couple of hours before bedtime now, and Elsie may be upset by the change in routine – but if they have any chance of securing a deal with Adler's, they have to take up their offer of a meeting soon. Jake will need to present at least four different flavours to demonstrate their versatility, and this is an opportunity she can't afford to mess up.

When she goes into the shop, the first thing she does is check that all the appliances are running as they should be. She reminded Jake again this morning that he needs to contact the company they'd bought the freezer from again, although what difference it'll make now she isn't sure. The damage is done. Jake has changed the fuse so the freezer is up and running again, but she's still having to start everything from scratch.

'We need a coffee before we do anything else,' Tyler suggests. He has kindly offered to be her apprentice for the morning, and he was there by 5 a.m. to complete all the early chores out on the farm.

'Good idea.' Natalie switches the coffee machine on and finds an unopened bag of roasted beans at the back of the cupboard. Most of the stock was used up before they closed for the winter, though she held back some supplies for personal consumption. Sometimes, when she gets a chance, she likes to come out here in the evening after Elsie's gone to sleep and sit alone with a drink and a book, the only time to herself she ever manages to get. During the winter months, though, it's often too cold, and she can't justify turning the heating on in here just for the sake of an hour's me-time.

'It'll be as good as the last batch,' Tyler tells her optimistically. 'If not better.'

She gives him a grateful smile as she sets about making the coffee. She appreciates his positivity, even when she feels it's misplaced. She likes having Tyler around; in truth, she doesn't know how the farm would function without him.

'How are things going with Kara?' he asks.

'Fine. Good. She's quiet; we barely notice she's here some days.'

'What job does she do?'

'Something in computers. Sounded pretty boring when she told me.'

'Seems a strange choice of place to live though. What's there around here for a city girl?'

Natalie shrugs. She doesn't want to mention Kara's father's death. 'You like it here.'

'I'm not a city girl.'

Natalie laughs and digs an elbow into his skinny ribs as she passes him to get to the fridge.

'Anyway,' Tyler says, 'I grew up around here. Same as you... I'm stuck.' He smiles as he says it, but the words still hit a nerve. Is this how he sees her life? How he sees all their lives? She'd always thought he was happy here, that he'd had no desire to leave. She feels her jaw tense as she stirs a sugar into Tyler's coffee.

'Talk to me,' he says, as he prepares the ice cream making machine. 'I always know when there's something wrong.'

'There's nothing to worry about,' she says, reaching for the freshly pasteurised milk she brought in earlier from the barn. 'I'm fine.'

He pulls a face. 'You can't kid a kidder.'

Natalie passes him the mug of coffee. 'I could have done without having to do this again.'

She enjoys the process of making ice cream, but not under these circumstances, not when she'd already made everything once and had produced what she'd thought was the best-tasting batch she'd ever made. She doesn't think she'll be that lucky twice in a row, but whatever she comes up with today is going to have to be good enough for Jake to pitch.

The thought of having to present anything in front of a team of supermarket executives makes her head spin. She's always been more than happy to let Jake take care of any aspect of the business that involves meeting and liaising with people: she would fall to pieces under that kind of pressure. Natalie knows where her comfort zones lie, and she's happy to remain within them.

She stops and puts a hand to her head, a dizzy spell making her lose her balance. She leans heavily against the cupboard. Tyler stops what he's doing and goes to her.

'This is fine then?' he says, raising an eyebrow.

'It's just a funny spell,' she says, too defensively. 'Is it me or is it boiling in here?'

'It's October,' Tyler reminds her, as Natalie pulls off her jumper. 'It's you.'

He returns to his task, keeping a watchful eye on her as she sets about her own. He has always been like an older brother to her, looking out for her and trying to keep her protected, even though there's only a matter of months in age between them. Whenever a boy showed her any interest at school, Tyler always seemed to know about it before Natalie, and when she first started going out with Jake, Tyler reacted to the relationship with a coldness Natalie's friends described as jealousy. He'd been used to having Natalie to himself. Now, he was going to have to share her.

'Is this to do with Tom's birthday?'

In just under a fortnight, Natalie's father would have been celebrating his fiftieth birthday. Every year that passes is difficult, but this one feels like a milestone. Her father died at forty, still a young man. He was fit and capable, running the farm almost single-handedly other than for the help he had from Jake and Tyler at weekends and after school. He was in good health. He had years ahead of him. And then a single few moments ended all their lives as they'd known them.

'Come here.'

Tyler goes back to Natalie, wincing as he puts his arms around her.

'Your leg?'

'Shhh,' he says, pulling her closer to him. He never talks about his injury. She knows how much it affects him – the doctors warned that he would have a lifelong weakness there –

and yet no one ever hears him complain of the pain she knows it sometimes causes him.

'I miss them,' she says into his chest.

'I know. I miss them too.'

'I wish I'd been there with them that day.'

Tyler holds her shoulders and gently pushes her back so he can look at her. 'Don't say that. Neither of them would have wanted that. I couldn't have faced losing you as well.'

Natalie looks at the deep scar that runs across Tyler's cheek. 'But you survived.'

'I was lucky. And I've never stopped feeling guilty for it.'

Natalie feels a pang of remorse in her chest, wishing she could swallow back her words. She has no idea of Tyler's recollections of that day or of the accident; they've rarely talked about it, Natalie never wanting to make him relive the horrors of what he must have seen that day, and Tyler in return never wanting to expose her to them. She doesn't envy him the solitude of his memories, or the survivor's guilt he lives with.

'They'd be proud of you,' he tells her, stepping away. 'You've got to always remember that.'

'I'm not so sure about that. The last few years have been a disaster.'

'They've not been a disaster. Things have been challenging, but they're not your fault. You couldn't help a pandemic or a TB outbreak. Not everything's in your control.'

He's right, she knows, and sometimes she hates the way Tyler sees things so pragmatically.

'Come on,' he says. 'Ice cream.'

They set about their separate tasks, Natalie preparing flavours while Tyler preps the equipment. She begins to feel queasy again, swallowing down the nausea, not wanting Tyler to know. He says something to her, but she doesn't hear what it is. Then she hears his voice repeating her name, the words increasingly distorted as though they are being spoken under water. She tries to speak back to him, to respond in some way, but her own voice is strangled, held back by a dizziness that rushes through her and lifts her legs from beneath her. And then she hits the floor, and the world turns black.

FOURTEEN

Elsie's sitting at the dining table, a pencil case of felt-tipped pens spilled out on top of her unicorn colouring book. The book itself seems to have escaped much of the colour, though the wooden tabletop's adorned with frantic scribbles of pinks and reds. However, while Elsie's quiet for a few moments it seems a small sacrifice to make. It isn't my table, and if she was my kid she'd never have been allowed to reach a stage where she thought that was acceptable behaviour.

I should be working, but I've found it difficult to concentrate today. Natalie's still at the hospital, being kept overnight as a precaution, and now she's there I feel I should do something productive, something that might help cement my permanence at the farm during her absence.

'What do you want for dinner?' Jake asks Elsie.

Elsie, away with the fairies ninety-five per cent of the time, doesn't answer, distracted by a pen lid she can't remove.

'Elsie. What do you want for dinner?'

Jake mutters something beneath his breath when his daughter yet again refuses to respond. She's been given too much freedom and not enough attention, that's the problem.

While Natalie's focus has been on the farm and her little ice cream project – and now on the extra job needed to compensate for the financial fuck-up the latter has proved to be – Elsie has been given too much space to roam, with no structure beyond her three mornings at nursery.

'I'll make dinner for her,' I offer.

Jake sighs and mumbles something inaudible beneath his breath. He looks at me, but he doesn't really. Too often recently he looks through me, hearing my voice but not connecting with the words I've spoken. It sometimes feels as though I'm losing him, yet when I've watched him with Natalie, it isn't too hard to see she feels the same. I don't believe for a moment we'd both lose him. Jake isn't that person. He can't be alone. He doesn't know life without the crutch of a partner.

'I'm just trying to help.'

'Well, don't.'

I stand close behind him and run a hand beneath his sweater, my fingertips skimming his taut stomach. His body reacts involuntarily, melting towards mine before he recoils and turns sharply to me, fighting every natural instinct.

'Don't.' He gestures to Elsie, who is still at the dining table, merrily circling a teacup stain with a black colouring pen.

'She hasn't seen anything.'

He goes to Elsie, kisses her on the top of her head and tells her to be a good girl while he's gone. He reassures her he won't be long and he'll be back in time to read to her before she goes to sleep.

'Spend the night with me,' I say as he heads to the porch.

'We can't,' he hisses.

'Or you won't.'

Jake grabs me by the arm, and I'm grateful for the reaction. It's something, at least. He's been so unresponsive recently his anger is preferable to his silence.

'Natalie's in hospital, for fuck's sake,' he says through gritted teeth. 'This is her home.'

'It's my home too.'

Jake grabs my arm. His fingers, strong and calloused from years of manual labour, dig into my skin. Hit me, I think. But I know he won't. That's not who he is.

'This isn't your home.'

'It isn't yours either, remember? How many times have you told me this place has never felt like home, not really?'

He pulls me into the porch at the side of the kitchen and shoves the door shut behind us, not wanting Elsie to overhear any more of the argument. Because that's what this is, and I wonder if this is what married life is like – continual ongoing resentment and recriminations. We wouldn't be like this, I tell myself. If we lived together – when we live together – we would understand each other. We're different.

'You're not going to leave her, are you?' I want to goad him, to keep him responding.

Jake's jaw has tightened. A vein throbs at his left temple. What looks like anger I realise now is no such thing: it's fear. He's a frightened animal, trapped in a cycle of domesticity, enslaved by a series of circumstances and wrong choices. This isn't the life he'd wanted, and he has no idea how he's going to escape.

'I told you I'd leave her and I will. But not yet. There are things I need to sort out here first, you know that. I can't just abandon the farm and I can't abandon Elsie. If I just up and leave I'll never get to see her.'

'Who said anything about going anywhere? We could stay here, and Elsie would stay with us.'

It's the first time I've ever mentioned Elsie staying with us, although a promise that I'll be accepting of her in our lives has always been what he's wanted to hear. On so many occasions he's brought his daughter into talk of our future, never explicitly stating that he wants the three of us together yet always offering enough of a hint that the life we have spoken of so frequently in the past includes Elsie there as a permanent presence.

'What are you talking about?' he asks, panic in his voice. I burn at his reaction. I thought he'd be happy at what I am suggesting. Isn't this what he's always wanted?

'You thought I was too scared to take Elsie on, and perhaps you were right, I was scared. I've never thought about being a parent, but I can do it – *we* can do this. The three of us, together.'

Jake's dark eyes narrow. 'And Natalie just hands over Elsie without argument? After finding out what we've been up to, she just says, "here we go then, take my daughter, too"?'

'It'll be hard, I know it will, but we can make it work.'

'She's her mother, for God's sake. We can't just take Elsie away from her.'

He won't look me in the eye. Here's the core of the problem he hasn't wanted to face up to or try to deal with: he doesn't want to be with Natalie, but he doesn't want to lose Elsie. The courts always favour the mother; there are plenty of examples to show that. The realisation that he loves his daughter more than he loves me stings. I will never get him away from this place while Elsie's still here and Natalie has parental control.

He looks at me directly now, eyes filled with tears. 'She'll stop me from ever seeing her again,' he whispers.

I take his face in my hands, his stubble rough against my palms, and I smooth his cheek with my thumb, as if I could work the worry from him like a genie being rubbed free from a lamp. 'That won't happen,' I try to reassure him. But it will. That's exactly what would happen.

'How do you know? She's going to hate me. She'll just take Elsie and I'll never see her again.'

'She won't. She can't just do that. You have rights too.'

'No one's going to side with a husband who's been having an affair.'

The door opens and I step back quickly, my hands falling from Jake's face.

'Daddy, I'm hungry.'

Elsie stands in the doorway, felt-tip pen in hand. She's scrawled some across her face, a long green line staining her cheek.

'I'll make you dinner,' I say cheerily, reaching out to take Elsie's hand. 'How about spaghetti bolognese? I know it's your favourite.' I lead her back to the kitchen, distracting her from Jake as he pulls himself together. 'You get back to your work,' I turn to say to him.

'Are you sure?' he says reluctantly.

I shrug nonchalantly, as though the last few minutes never happened. 'It's not a problem. I'm happy to help in whatever way I can; you know that.' I smile at him, but the look goes unreturned.

Once he's gone, I set about preparing bolognese, finding an onion in the vegetable rack and some garlic in the door of the fridge. Elsie moves from the table to her little wooden kitchen in the corner, mimicking my actions as I peel and chop.

'Where's Mummy?'

'She's at the hospital.'

'Is she sick?'

'She's okay. She'll be home soon.'

I pour oil into a frying pan and watch as it heats, waiting for the pops and cracks as it becomes too hot. Jake's words echo in my head. *She'll take Elsie away, I'll never see her again.* I couldn't tell him how I know this will never happen, or how my plan to free us from the problem of Natalie has already been put into place.

I look over my shoulder at Elsie, who's grown tired of chopping wooden halves of vegetables and is now instead loading them all into a little plastic shopping basket. Mummy will be okay, I think. For now. The dosage of sleeping tablets I gave her, along with the extra antidepressants, wasn't enough to keep her out of action for long, but next time, who knows, she may be incapacitated a little longer. Long enough to prove she's an unfit mother to Elsie, and long enough to make sure Jake finally leaves her.

FIFTEEN

When Jake brings Natalie home from the hospital the house is spotless. They go in through the front door, which is rarely used, and the hallway smells of furniture polish and the enormous white and pink lilies that have been arranged in a glass vase on the side table. When she goes into the living room there's bunting above the fireplace, the words 'Welcome Home' traced over with Elsie's wobbly writing.

'Thank you,' Natalie says, turning to Jake with a grateful smile. She still feels shaky despite being rested. The hospital put the collapse down to exhaustion and stress, and had it not been for the bump to the head when she'd hit the ground she would have been sent home the same day and not needed to be kept in. She's had a headache ever since she fell, though they've been plaguing her for weeks already.

'I can't take any credit for anything,' he says. 'Kara's done most of it.'

Natalie feels her stomach twist. When she came in and saw how much had been done, all the effort that had been made, she'd felt uplifted; now, knowing it's Kara and not Jake who's responsible, her reaction feels different. She thinks of Kara cleaning her house, judging the state of the place as she moved things to vacuum the carpets; she imagines her going through their things, scathing of how disorganised and chaotic their home is. She pictures Kara sitting with Elsie, the two of them chatting and laughing as they made bunting together, and a stab of jealousy pierces her gut.

'Are you hungry?' Jake asks. 'Kara's made a shepherd's pie if you fancy it.'

Natalie's anxiety balloons in her chest. During her brief stay in hospital she had plenty of time to think, and the more thinking she did, the worse her anxiety became. Everything that flooded her brain on the evening she fell comes back to her now, her deepest fears gathered around her. She remembers Jake and Kara sitting together on the sofa, drinking wine like old friends or worse, like lovers; she recalls the evening she tried to instigate intimacy with him, only to be rejected. Suddenly, the room no longer looks as welcoming as it did moments ago.

'I don't really fancy anything. I'm sorry, I'm still so tired. Where's Elsie?'

'Playing in the barn with Tyler. I'll go and tell them you're here.'

Natalie watches Jake leave and sits on the sofa. Before she left the hospital, one of the nurses told her she should spend the next couple of days resting up, but she knows that's the last thing she can afford to do. While she's been away anything might have happened, and if something wasn't already going on between Jake and Kara, it's now been given a chance to take root.

'It's good to see you back.' Natalie turns to see Kara in the doorway, a mug of tea in her hand and a smile on her face. Acting, Natalie thinks, and she wonders whether the performance began the moment she first visited the house.

'Thank you,' she manages politely, swallowing the lump of disgust that's sat like bile in her throat.

She is being ridiculous, she realises that. Jake isn't an idiot, and to start an affair with a woman living in their home would be lunacy. It would be marriage suicide. He would never gamble with their family like that... would he?

'How are you feeling?'

'Much better,' she lies.

'What do they think caused it? Jake said the doctors said it was probably stress.'

Natalie feels herself growing hot beneath her sweater. Jake's been discussing her with Kara, telling her private details that should have stayed between them. Have they laughed at her behind her back, wondering how she can be such a fool? Perhaps he feels guilty, though if he does, he can't possibly feel guilty enough. She would never be capable of doing what he's doing. They're supposed to be a team; that's how it's always been.

'Possibly. But I'm fine now. Just one of those things.'

She was questioned by the doctors about her medication after her blood test results came back and they'd picked up on the antidepressants and sleeping tablets she's been taking since her late teens. Could she have accidentally overdosed? they'd asked her, but, in all the time she's been using them, she's been vigilant in her routine. Yet she'd noticed last week that she seemed to have fewer pills left than she'd thought. She didn't mention it to Jake, knowing he would have dismissed it as her forgetfulness. And perhaps he would have been right. So much has been going on that it isn't unthinkable she may have made a mistake.

'Do you have any family living locally?'

Natalie wonders where the question has come from. Kara seems to be taking too much interest all of a sudden. Or maybe she's trying to be helpful.

'You just seem to be under so much pressure with the farm and looking after Elsie. I wondered if you ever get a break.'

'Jake's parents are only a twenty-minute drive away. But they're both still working and busy. We don't really see much of them.'

Natalie tries to keep resentment from her voice. It's hard to talk of her in-laws without feeling the tricky tangle of emotions that always knots in her stomach at the thought of them. They've never liked her, and never made a secret of the fact. As far as they're concerned, Natalie held their son back from moving on to bigger and better things, despite the fact that it was Natalie who'd secured a university place. Jake rarely mentions his parents, and, on the few occasions Natalie does, he quickly changes the subject. She'd hoped when she'd got pregnant that a grandchild might bring them together, but even Elsie hasn't been enough for them to want to bridge the gap.

'You and Jake must never get any time together, just the two of you.'

'We see each other occasionally after Elsie's asleep. By which time either one or both of us is exhausted and ready for bed.'

'If you ever want a night out, I'd be happy to babysit. As long as Elsie's okay with it.'

'Thank you. That's really nice of you.' Natalie doesn't know where she is with this woman. One moment she suspects her of being involved with her husband; the next, she's grateful for her kindness. And it is a kind offer, but one Natalie knows she would never take Kara up on. There are few people she trusts to look after Elsie.

Her attention's distracted for a moment by the mantelpiece. It has been polished – she knows this because the ornaments arranged there have been moved from their usual places. Her parents' clock still stands in the middle, but the vase to the right now rests precariously close to the edge, and the framed photographs of Elsie are sitting in a different order to how Natalie usually has them. And then there's the pot that holds her parents' wedding rings: a gift given to them on their wedding day by an elderly aunt who died when Natalie was a child. It isn't there.

'Did you clean?'

'I thought it would be nice for you to come home to. I'm sorry, have I done something wrong?'

'The pot on the mantelpiece,' Natalie says, getting up and going to the fireplace. 'Where is it?'

'What pot?'

Natalie eyes Kara with suspicion. Is she lying when she claims not to know what she's referring to? Kara doesn't spend much time in the living room; at least, she doesn't spend much time there when Natalie's home. Who knows how frequently she might be there during the three evenings a week when Natalie is working at the pub? Only Kara. And Jake.

'The blue pot.' She raises a hand and makes a gesture to demonstrate its size. 'This big.'

'I haven't seen it,' Kara tells her.

'It was there. It's always there. Did you dust the mantelpiece?'

'Yes, but—'

'Then it would have been there.'

'It wasn't,' Kara says. 'I don't remember seeing a blue pot there. Everything that was there I just picked up and put back.'

'Is something the matter?' Jake comes into the living room with Elsie, who rushes to Natalie when she sees her home.

Natalie crouches to cuddle her, grateful for the familiar warmth and comfort of her daughter's small body. She nuzzles her face into her hair, trying not to think about Kara and Jake; trying to push away the unwanted thoughts of them together that keep working their way into her consciousness.

'The pot with my parents' wedding rings in is missing.'

Jake looks to the mantelpiece. 'It must be here somewhere. It can't have just disappeared.'

'But it has.'

'I'll help you look for it,' Kara offers.

'It's fine. I'll do it. Come on, Elsie.'

Natalie takes her daughter by the hand and leads her out of the living room. Midway to the kitchen she pauses, waiting to overhear any exchange between Jake and Kara. But there's nothing other than talk of the pot and what it looks like, and Kara reiterating that it wasn't there when she dusted the mantelpiece. Natalie takes Elsie to the kitchen and plays with her for a while, getting Elsie to make her pretend cups of tea and slices of cake served on spotted plastic saucers.

Of all the things that could go missing, why the ring pot? It isn't a coincidence. The thought of losing the rings makes Natalie's insides flips. They're of no great monetary value, but they are precious to her, and she was hoping to pass them on to Elsie when she's old enough to appreciate and take care of them.

Jake comes into the kitchen. 'You okay?'

'Not really. You know that pot doesn't move... it's always on the mantelpiece; it's been there for years.'

'Kara says she didn't see it.'

'I think she should go.'

'What?'

'I don't think Kara should stay here any longer. I'd like her to leave.'

Jake sighs. 'You were the one who was keen to have her here. It's barely been a fortnight... you haven't given her a chance.'

'You've changed your tune. So you want her here now?'

'We need the money, remember? And apart from that, she's good to have around.'

Natalie raises an eyebrow. 'Really?'

'Yes, really. I've seen how much she tries to help around the house. It takes pressure off us both.'

She meets his eye and holds his gaze, hoping for some sign of guilt. 'The pot was on the mantelpiece.'

'I'll keep an eye out for it. I'd better get back to work. Kara's not going anywhere, okay?'

When he goes back out onto the farm, Natalie takes Elsie upstairs. She searches her bedroom for the pot, but she knows it won't be there; Elsie is too little to reach the mantelpiece, so she wouldn't have been able to take it even had she tried to. She goes to her own bedroom, leaving Elsie to play with her doll's house. She searches through the drawers and on top of the dressing table, in the wardrobe and on the windowsill; anywhere the pot might have been put and forgotten. She begins to question herself: had she moved it for some reason? Did she take it from the mantelpiece when Kara moved in, not wanting to risk the rings being lost?

She gets up and goes to the bathroom where she opens the cupboard and takes out her own medication. She has been taking Sertraline for almost a decade now, needing it to take the edge off her worries and overactive mind, yet here she is, worse than ever, and isn't this what it's supposed to prevent? She doesn't see the point in taking the pills if they no longer serve their purpose.

Maybe they're the problem, she thinks. What if the medication's stopping her seeing things clearly, preventing her from functioning in the way she should – in the way she needs to? She sits on the edge of the bath as she pulls out each individual blister strip and pushes each pill from behind the foil packaging, watching them pop out into the toilet. When everything is emptied, she flushes them away.

SIXTEEN

Natalie is out, at work at the pub. Her mood since she got back from the hospital has been increasingly fractious, fluctuating between irritability, anger and exhaustion, and the extra medication is having the desired effect. It was easy enough to do. Natalie's stash of both prescribed and over-the-counter medication is so extensive she hasn't noticed a couple of missing boxes. A coffee here, a glass of wine there, they have been easy enough to administer. Now that's she been admitted to hospital, her blood test results will have been recorded. The doctors already suspect she may have accidentally taken too many of her antidepressants, and someone able to confuse a dosage of medication would presumably be deemed a person in a fragile state of mind. They must think Natalie's exhausted and under pressure.

When I finish work I go into the living room, where Jake and Elsie are sitting side by side on sofa, tucked under a blanket and watching a film. I watch them for a moment, both of them unaware of my presence.

'Doggy!' Elsie says excitedly, pointing at the screen, and I wonder how many times the word has been spoken since the film started.

'Dalmatians,' Jake tells her.

'He's sad.'

'I know. The nasty woman's taken them away from their mummy, but it'll all be okay. She'll get them back.'

Jake is a good man; despite everything he's done, I still believe that. He's a better person than I am. He has always tried to do the best he can for everyone, but in trying to please other people he's sacrificed so much of himself. When I look at him now all I see is sadness. He deserves to be happy. I deserve to be happy.

'This looks like a scene that needs popcorn,' I say, and Jake turns to the sound of my voice. 'Is there any here?'

'Maybe in the cupboard next to the fridge.'

I go to the kitchen and find a bag of popcorn which I open out into a big plastic bowl, and I get Jake and me both a bottle of beer.

'Thanks,' Jake says, when I return to the living room. Elsie omits a squeal of excitement when I put the bowl of popcorn next to her, and she tucks in like a child who hasn't been fed for a week.

'Two minutes,' I say, looking at Jake with a raised eyebrow and nodding towards the door.

He puts his beer on the coffee table next to mine and follows me to the hallway. I guide him away from the doorway so we're out of Elsie's view before pushing his unruly hair from his face and kissing him.

'Natalie okay?'

He winces at her name. He doesn't like it when I talk about her, though it can hardly be avoided. 'Tired. The hospital told her she needs to ease up a bit. I've told her to quit the job at the pub but she won't listen.'

'I fucked someone else.'

I watch his face crumple as he registers my words, the shock so intense that he might have been hit with them. He backs away from me, but he's got nowhere to go.

'I don't understand,' he finally says.

'What's not to understand? That night I told you and Natalie I was meeting with an old friend: I met up with another man. We had sex. It was good.'

I wait for him to say something, but he can't or won't. His jaw tightens and his eyes stay fixed on mine, an initial response of disbelief quickly morphing into something that resembles hurt. It's always difficult to tell with Jake. He's closed so much of himself off to the world for so long that he sometimes seems to not know how to feel anything. I want to hurt him. I want him to burn with the same jealousy I've endured for so long now, because it's the only way I'm going to make him act.

'What?' I say, raising my hands and shrugging with a pretence at nonchalance. 'We're not exclusive, are we? You're still married, remember?'

We've never had the conversation of whether or not I sleep with other people; it has never been needed, and Jake has taken for granted that I won't have sex with anyone else. I've been his for as long as I'm able to remember. Sleeping with another man didn't make me feel good; in fact, it made me feel worse. But sometimes bad deeds are necessary.

Now, for the first time, I notice the tears he's trying to hold back. The elation I just felt at having him finally respond to something with some emotion is momentarily replaced with a flicker of regret, but I snuff it out as easily as a lit candle, returning my heart to darkness. I had to do it. In all the time we've been together, I've never done anything like that before. This is what he's brought me to. I'm just so tired of waiting. I'm so tired of hanging on for something that seems to be forever slipping further from my grip.

'How could you do that?' he finally asks.

'What's the difference? You go upstairs and you have sex with Natalie, don't you? How often do you two do it? Do you think of me when you fuck her?'

'Were you thinking of me when you fucked this other man?'

'Every second.'

It isn't the reply he was expecting, and I can't tell whether the surprise or the hurt on his face is the stronger of the two reactions. He is crying now, unashamed, his cheeks wet with tears. There's part of me that hates myself for what I've done, but he gave me no other choice.

Jake grabs my arm again. His fingers grip my skin, digging in. The veins at his left temple throb with anger, but there's something else: a flame that passes through him, banishing the nonchalance that usually resides behind his eyes.

'Hit me,' I tell him.

'What?'

'Hit me. Go on. Just do it.'

'Don't be stupid.'

'Come on,' I goad him.

'Stop it,' he snaps. 'Please. Just stop it.'

'Daddy.'

Elsie's voice breaks through the tension. He goes into the living room and talks to her calmly, his voice completely changed. We are actors, all of us, everyone in this house pretending to be something they're not. How easily the anger falls from his voice when he's speaking to his daughter. He's as much of a fraud as I am.

When he does come back to me, he takes charge. He reaches for my face and holds it in his hands before nudging a leg between mine and pushing me against the wall. He kisses me urgently, his tongue finding mine. He's picturing the other man; he feels a need to make a point now. I know how torturous it is, to be forced to imagine the person you love with someone else, knowing that they're there with them and there's nothing you can do to stop it from happening. I have lived this torment over and over.

My hands find his zip, but he stops me before I can undo it. 'I wish you hadn't done it,' he says quietly.

'Me too. And I'm sorry.' I kiss him again. 'Do you love me?'

'You know I do.'

'Then prove it.'

He glances to the living room. 'Let me put Elsie to bed.'

I move away from him and we go back into the living room together. Elsie has fallen asleep on the sofa, her head lolled awkwardly on the arm rest, and I watch Jake as he scoops her up and carries her, limbs dangly, up to bed. He'll come back down in a minute: he'll undress me; we'll fuck on the sofa as we've done so many times before. But it won't prove anything. This isn't love; it's just sex, and it doesn't mean anything if it isn't backed by a promise. If he wants to prove he loves me, Jake is going to have to do a whole lot more.

SEVENTEEN

The following Thursday, Jake goes to Bristol to meet with the buying team at Adler's. She hasn't told him that she got rid of her medication; she knows what his reaction is likely to be, and besides, he would want to know the reason for it. His trip coincides with what would have been her father's birthday – October 31st – and though Jake tells her he feels he should be with her on that day, Natalie insists that he goes. They need this contract. If the fuse in the plug hadn't failed, the meeting would have already been and gone, but it was no one's fault and it can't be helped. They can't afford to lose this opportunity.

Tyler tells Natalie not to plan anything for dinner, and at 6.30 p.m. he calls her and Elsie into the kitchen.

'I'm sorry it's late for her tea,' he apologies. 'But I thought with it being Halloween a late night might be a treat.'

He stands aside and holds out an arm like a magician about to pull off an impossible feat of illusion. On the dining table, the contents of a Chinese takeaway have been laid out like a skeleton corpse, complete with sticky ribs and noodle intestines. BBQ sauce has been strategically placed to resemble blood.

'Oh my God,' laughs Natalie. 'That's so gross.'

'Kids love gross.'

Elsie runs up to the table and swipes a spring roll bone from the corpse's finger.

'I also have these,' Tyler says, turning to the worktop behind him and grabbing a bag of Braeburns. 'I thought we could do bobbing for apples.'

'Yay!' Elsie shouts, though Natalie isn't sure whether she even understands what bobbing for apples involves. She hates even having water splashed on her face when she's in the bath.

'Thank you,' Natalie says to Tyler. She looks back at the table. 'This is a lot of food though.'

'Yeah... I might have over-ordered. Is Kara about? She could help us.'

'She's gone out for the evening.'

'Save the rest for when Jake gets home tomorrow then. It's always nicer the day after.'

They eat together, Elsie gorging on spring rolls and chicken balls until she gets so full that she collapses onto her mother's lap. Tyler gets a mixing bowl from one of the cupboards, fills it with water and demonstrates to Elsie how to bob for apples – something she finds hilarious once the front of his hair and T-shirt are soaking.

After clearing up, they go into the living room and Natalie puts *101 Dalmatians*, Elsie's current favourite film, on the television. Elsie snuggles in between Natalie and Tyler, food-drunk and exhausted by the fun and, before Cruella de Vil has had a chance to steal the puppies, Elsie's fallen asleep with her head in her mother's lap.

'She okay?' Tyler asks, when Natalie returns from carrying Elsie up to bed.

'Wiped out. Thank you for tonight, she loved it. So did I.'

'I've bought some fireworks for next week too. I thought we could do our own little display in the garden.' He gestures to his beer. 'I'm not going to offer you one.'

'But I'll have one.'

'Really?'

'One beer won't hurt, will it?'

Tyler eyes her with a concern that manages to feel over-bearing.

'It's one bottle of beer,' she tells him. 'For Dad.'

He gets up and goes to the kitchen, returning with a bottle he hands to her. He holds out his own bottle and clinks the top of it against hers. 'Happy birthday, Tom.'

'Happy birthday, Dad.'

They each take a sip. Other than the wine she shared with Kara over dinner a couple of weeks back, it's the first alcohol she's had in as long as she's able to remember, and it goes straight to her head. She's vowed to keep her mind clear, but Jake is away and Kara's out; there's nothing she has to do tonight. Then the thought hits her like a punch to the head. What if Kara is with him?

She can't be, she tells herself. Jake left hours ago, and Kara went out just a short while later, without any overnight things. She could have hidden them somewhere, the suspicious voice in her head tells her. Or Jake could have taken them with him for her when he left.

Natalie picks up her beer and swigs back half the bottle. Two voices in her brain argue between themselves: one fighting the rational argument that they wouldn't do something so blatantly obvious, while the other tries to convince her that Jake and Kara are currently in a hotel bed having the kind of sex she and Jake used to have back when they were teenagers.

'Where have you gone, Natalie?'

He knows her too well, she thinks. Better, sometimes it seems, than Jake knows her. 'Nowhere.'

'Liar.'

She drags herself from thoughts of Jake and what he might now be doing. 'I was just thinking about that time Dad took us trick or treating in the village, do you remember? And he made that fake child with the Guy Fawkes clothing?'

Tyler laughs at the memory. 'No one except Mrs Davies at the Post Office dared to challenge him on the mysterious "cousin" we were dragging down the high street. Miserable old cow.'

Natalie laughs. The memory is bittersweet.

'I'm going to get another beer,' Tyler says.

'And one for me, please. And if you don't get it, I'll just get it myself, so you're saving me the trip.'

She's already had enough; Natalie knows she should stop now. She can feel the slow tug of the alcohol at her brain that's warning her not to have any more. She should tell Tyler she's tired, give the hint for him to go, yet she realises she doesn't want him to. It's been a lovely evening and she's for once enjoying herself; it's nice having him here, having someone who actually listens to her.

'What's the matter?'

He's known her too long for her to be able to hide much from him. There might have been a time she could talk to him about anything, but things aren't so simple any more, though. Tyler is also Jake's closest friend; she can't confide in him with her suspicions.

'Natalie?'

Tears spark at the corners of her eyes. Embarrassed, she presses her fingertips to her skin, willing herself to hold back from tipping over into the kind of emotional outpouring she and Tyler have always tended to veer away from.

Beer bottle still in hand, Tyler moves to the sofa and sits next to her. His thigh touches hers, and when he reaches to put his free hand on her arm, her skin reacts with a sheen of goosebumps. The cold, she thinks, confused by the involuntary response to his touch. It's just the cold. The alcohol.

'You can tell me anything, you know that. So what is it?'

'I can't though, can I? I can't tell you *every*thing.'

Tyler's grey eyes fix themselves on her as he reaches to push her hair behind her ear. The moment lasts too long; the intimacy too intense. 'It's to do with Jake?'

She nods.

'He's my friend,' Tyler says, his hand sliding to her arm. 'But you're my family first. What's happened?'

Natalie moves her gaze from his. She feels him continue to stare at her, his gaze warming her skin. He looks different tonight, somehow. Or maybe it's just the way he's looking at her that's different. She can't remember the last time Jake looked at her like Tyler is now. Perhaps she made the wrong choice all those years ago, she thinks. Maybe she picked the wrong friend.

Then she shakes herself quickly from the thought, shamed by it.

'I think he's having an affair.'

He half smiles, disbelieving. 'Why would you think that?'

Natalie wonders whether Jake might have already confided in him about an affair. Would he trust Tyler with that kind of secret?

'He's been so distant recently. And I know there's been a lot going on with Elsie and the farm and everything, but this feels like something more. He never touches me – he won't go near me. And I just know him. I know he's keeping something from me.'

'You've both been under so much pressure,' Tyler says, moving his hand from her arm as he sits back. 'You're both exhausted with worry, about Elsie, the cattle, money – everything. Jake loves you, Natalie. He would never look at another woman.'

It sounds so easy to believe when he says it. When she thinks about it rationally and tries to organise the chaos of her thoughts, common sense tells Natalie that even if Jake was tempted by the idea of an affair, his opportunities for carrying one out have been minimal. There have been the trips to agri-cultural shows that have involved occasional nights away, but they have been few and far between. But that was enough time, her doubts tell her. Sufficient to have met someone and for something to have been started.

'Where's he gone?' she asks, her thoughts making her dizzy.

Tyler pulls a face. He has a thin top lip that gets sucked between his teeth whenever he's concentrating or considering something, and it does so now, his focus lost to something Natalie cannot see. She begins to analyse the gesture, wondering whether his brain is busy formulating the lie that's about to slip from his lips or whether tiredness and stress have finally pushed her into the territory of paranoia.

'He's gone to pitch your ice cream. *For you.* You know that.'

'Do I?' Natalie says, her mind racing ahead of her. 'How do I know though, really? I'm not there, am I? He could come back tomorrow and tell me, sorry, Nat, I tried my best but they didn't want to make an offer, when he never really went to any meeting at all. He might be in a hotel room with someone else right now, laughing at how stupid I am.'

She won't mention Kara. She doesn't want Tyler to know what she suspects, and she won't bring her into it until she's got proof.

Tyler drains his bottle before returning it to the wooden trestle table that rests at the end of the sofa. 'You should write a film script... that sounds quite gripping.' He moves closer to her again, putting a reassuring hand on her knee. 'You need more sleep. That's all this is. We should call it a night. I'm sorry, I shouldn't have stayed so late.' And then his fingers tighten their hold, passing the silent message that he doesn't really want to go.

The moment seems to stretch between them, too silent yet somehow too loud. The house feels big and too empty, and Jake feels a million miles away. It wouldn't be right, Natalie tells herself. Two wrongs would only make everything worse, and this is Tyler... he's always been like a brother to her.

She's grateful when he gets up, the moment broken. She follows him to the hallway, where he puts on his jacket.

'You sure you'll be okay walking back to the village?'

He laughs. 'I'm a big boy. I'm sure I'll be fine.'

He gives her a kiss on the cheek and tells her to stop worrying, and she wishes she could believe him, but for once she can't take any comfort from his optimism. When he leaves, she goes back to the living room. She drains the last of the beer from the bottle and turns on the television, desperate for distraction from thoughts of Jake.

* * *

When Natalie wakes, disorientated, she can't remember falling asleep, and she wonders what she's doing still in the living room. Her neck is cricked from sleeping with her head at an awkward angle, and when she gets up she feels a shooting pain that drives up to her brain. It is so cold. She goes upstairs and uses the bathroom before heading to her bedroom, but before she gets there she notices Elsie's bedroom door's open. She always closes it after getting her to sleep; not fully, but enough that the light from the landing doesn't bother her.

Natalie's heart skips as she goes into her daughter's room. Her eyes take a moment to adjust to the darkness. When they do, she sees that Elsie isn't there.

'Elsie. Elsie!'

Panic rips through her. Natalie searches the room, even looking beneath the bed, but her daughter is nowhere to be found.

'Elsie!' She rushes back out onto the landing, going into every other room and turning on all the lights. When she goes back downstairs, she stops dead at the foot of the staircase, stalled by something she hadn't noticed when she'd left the living room earlier. The front door is open.

She pulls on a pair of trainers and rushes onto the driveway, calling her daughter's name into the night air. Scenes from a nightmare play out in front of her in the darkness: Elsie trampled by one of the cattle; Elsie injured by a piece of farming machinery. The harder she screams, the weaker her voice seems to become, lost on the sharp pull of the wind. She's crying now, tears streaking her face as she checks the garden before running to the barns.

'Elsie!'

This can't be happening, she tells herself, the words repeated over and over, the only thing to keep her sane. Her love for her daughter swells like a tumour in her chest, so big it feels capable of bursting through her ribcage. She gives up on the barns and goes back to the driveway, where she's met with the darkness that leads to the gate of the farm's main entrance. It's open. The lanes, she thinks, sick at the thought. Elsie might have wandered out onto the lanes.

Natalie runs faster than she ever has, her heart pounding in her chest; her body numb with the cold. The lanes are much darker than the driveway, sheltered from the sky by an archway of trees that hangs over the tarmac, and Natalie wishes now that she'd had the presence of mind to bring her phone. She could have used the torch. But it's too late to turn around and get it now. What if Elsie's out here alone? She doesn't have time to lose.

As she rounds the second bend in the lane, Natalie sees a figure ahead of her. Her body jolts to a halt, terrified by a silhouette whose shape she can't distinguish. It's too tall to be a child, but its outline isn't that of a person, too extended at the sides, too star-shaped to be human. It's walking towards her, and as it nears she realises it isn't a person. It is two people. An adult carrying a child. She races towards them, and as she nears her eyes allow her to see now for the first time what and who is ahead of her. Kara. Kara carrying Elsie.

'Elsie!'

Natalie hears a moan from her daughter's lips and her stomach flips with relief. She's alive, she thinks. But she has no idea whether or not she is harmed.

'What are you doing with her?'

Elsie hangs limply in Kara's arms, the sequins of her princess pyjamas caught by the streaks of moonlight that glint through the trees overhead. Natalie grabs her daughter from Kara's arms, relief settling in her gut with the weight of her warm body. She feels sick at the thought of the empty bed and the opened door. She is crushed by the echo of what might have happened. A nauseating concoction of alcohol, fear and guilt churns in her stomach. Elsie's wide eyes stare up at her, confused yet trusting. Natalie doesn't deserve her trust. She's supposed to look after her, make sure she is kept safe. Always.

'Are you okay, sweetheart? Are you hurt?'

Elsie makes a small noise like a mewling cat before turning into her mother's chest and hiding her face.

'I was on my way home,' Kara says. There's a brittleness to her voice; she is affronted by the unspoken accusation that landed between them with Natalie's question.

'From where?'

'I met up with a friend.'

'What friend?' Natalie asks brusquely. 'You don't know anyone around here.' She regrets the words as soon as they're spoken – or at least, she regrets her tone. This isn't Kara's fault, she reminds herself. It's *hers*. Elsie is her responsibility.

'I don't think she's hurt,' Kara says, reaching out to stroke the back of Elsie's hair. 'But she was limping when I found her. She might have twisted her ankle. And you're welcome, by the way.'

In the darkness, Natalie feels her face flush with shame.

What sort of mother allows this to happen? What sort of mother drinks too much and leaves a door unlocked so that her young child's able to wander from her bed and end up on a road in the middle of the night?

She grips Elsie to her chest and buries her head in her hair, hiding her tears from Kara. She wonders whether she'll tell Jake what's happened tonight. If she does, she knows he will never forgive her.

EIGHTEEN

At just gone 3 a.m., I return to Elsie's room. She's sleeping peacefully, as she was when I came in earlier, her hands tucked beneath the side of her head as though in some form of prayer. The doll she carries everywhere with her has fallen onto the floor; I pick it up from the carpet and assess it for a moment. The next time Elsie sees her again – *if* she sees her again – little Loulou isn't going to look quite so clean.

I passed by Natalie's room on the way here, listening at the door to make sure I could hear her sleeping. Her breathing was heavy, so I'm confident she won't be woken too easily. There's enough time for me to sit here for a moment beside Elsie and watch her as she sleeps. There's plenty of time for me to plant a few seeds of doubt in her ear.

The longer a person's told something, the more they grow to believe it. Little Elsie already knows her mother is unwell – she knows she went to the hospital, and she knows she needs a lot of rest. Tomorrow, she will remember that her mother wasn't there for her when she needed her most. That it was another woman who carried her to safety. The memories of the night's events will come back gradually, creeping into her consciousness; once there, they'll have space to grow and fix themselves, more likely to stay forever.

And for now, I begin to tell her all the other things she needs to learn.

'Mummy doesn't love you,' I whisper close to her ear. Her body may be resting, but her subconscious is still awake: she will hear my words and silently absorb them; she will remember them in one form or another, though she may not recall where she heard them.

'Mummy left the door open. Mummy let you walk out into the lanes on your own. Anything might have happened. A car might have hit you. Mummy isn't fit to look after you. You're not safe with her.'

I reach across her sleeping body and tuck a stray strand of hair behind her ear. She responds to the touch, nuzzling her cheek against her pillow. She's aware. She'll absorb this.

'Mummy doesn't love you,' I say again. 'She's too tired. She's too poorly. Mummy's mind isn't right.'

The soft plush doll that rests on the duvet now stares at me accusingly. I snatch it away and stand gently, careful not to make any sound. I take the doll downstairs with me and out into the night, back down the lane where I earlier carried a sleeping Elsie. I find a spot by the roadside where it won't go missed by the headlights of a passing car, and I dump it face-down near the hedgerow. Jake will be home later today before anyone leaves the farm. Elsie isn't in nursery on Fridays, so Natalie won't have any reason to go out in the car. Traffic is so sparse on these lanes that the chance of anyone driving past before midday is unlikely, and even if they do, no one else would stop to retrieve a fallen doll from the roadside. Only someone who recognised it would bother about it, and when Jake sees it there he'll know it instantly. He'll pull the car over to collect it; he'll wonder what Elsie was doing here, and why the doll, her favourite, that never leaves the house for fear that she might get lost, was doing here, abandoned. He's going to ask questions Natalie isn't going to want to answer, but there'll be no way around it.

NINETEEN

Elsie wakes up early and goes into her parents' bedroom. She's usually a deep sleeper and often manages a twelve-hour stretch without disturbance, but the trauma of the previous evening's events have disrupted her sleep and at 5.30 a.m. she stands disorientated in the doorway, a fluffy brown teddy bear clutched to her chest. The duvet is pushed aside, and when she clambers up onto the bed, Natalie pulls it over them both and snuggles her daughter to her body.

'Where's Daddy?'

'He'll be back later.'

Too soon, Natalie thinks. She is either going to have to admit to Jake what happened the previous night or she's going to have to lie, and neither of these things is an appealing prospect. If she tells him, he's going to think her unfit to look after their child; he won't trust her alone with Elsie any more. If she doesn't tell him, she will run the risk of him finding out from someone else. She needs to talk to Kara, to make sure she doesn't talk to him about what happened.

Thoughts of Kara jolt any last vestiges of tiredness from her; she's awake now, fraught with the memory of seeing her with

Elsie in the lane just hours earlier. Where exactly had Kara been? With Jake, she thinks, though Jake was miles away, in Bristol. Or was he? Her mind starts circling again. She leans over to the bedside table and reaches for her phone, but it isn't there. Instead, her fingertips touch something smooth and solid, and when she turns to look she sees the blue pot sitting on the bedside table – the pot that had gone missing from the mantelpiece.

She sits up sharply and grabs the pot, opening it to check the rings are still inside. They are. But the pot wasn't there last night, she's sure of that. She would have seen it there when she came up to bed; she would have noticed it earlier in the day. Or would she? Natalie bites her lip with shame. She doesn't know that. She can't feel sure of anything that did or didn't happen last night.

Elsie rubs her eyes with a fist.

'Try to go back to sleep for a bit.'

But Elsie is wriggly and fidgety, her mind too active for her body to find rest. 'Loulou,' she says suddenly.

'Have you left her in your room?' Natalie asks through a yawn.

'She's gone.'

Natalie runs a hand through her daughter's blonde hair, her fingers getting tangled in a knot. Her face is changing, she thinks, the soft baby features she still had as a toddler replaced with the more defined features of a little girl. It's too soon. She wishes she could freeze time and keep Elsie as she is in this moment.

'Do you want to get her?'

'She's gone,' Elsie says again, frustrated this time.

'She can't be gone... she must be somewhere.' Natalie pushes the duvet off her. It's a cold morning, and the biting air nips through her pyjamas. The old stone farmhouse has always been cold; as a child, Natalie had been used to it, but she is beginning to feel it more and more.

'Come on,' she says, reaching out to lift Elsie from the bed. 'Let's go and find her.'

But Elsie is right: Loulou isn't in her bedroom. Natalie looks beneath the bed and under the duvet and pillow, inside the wardrobe and behind the toy box. The longer she looks, the more irritable Elsie becomes.

'You must have left her downstairs.'

Elsie follows Natalie to the living room, moaning all the while about wanting her doll back. When Natalie looks at the sofa, she's reminded of the exchange that passed between Tyler and her the night before, her leg brushing against his as they sat side by side. The thought that she might have chosen him instead of Jake when they were teenagers. She feels a flush of shame at the blurred memory.

Using Loulou as a distraction, Natalie searches the living room despite already knowing it isn't there – she's sure she would have seen it last night. Or would she? Her memories of last night are disjointed, as though she'd drunk two bottles of wine rather than a few beers. She regrets drinking. It was irresponsible after what happened little over a week ago. But she'd just wanted to feel normal for a while. Now, everything feels ten times worse.

Elsie cries when the doll isn't found. Natalie takes her to the kitchen to make her breakfast, but even her favourite chocolate cereal can't persuade her to abandon her heartbreak for a few minutes. She holds her daughter while she sobs, the guilt of what happened last night still hot and coarse inside her. She will make it up to her, she thinks, though she isn't yet sure how.

It's just past 10 a.m. when Jake comes through the front door. Natalie hadn't expected him until the afternoon; how often was it that he got a night away in a hotel, and why wouldn't he want to make the most of a double bed to himself and a full breakfast? Why wouldn't he want to make the most of his time with whoever he'd been with?

He nudges his small suitcase aside with his leg and takes off his jacket before hanging it over the banister.

'You're back early.'

'Nothing to hang about for. I wanted to get back.'

Maybe he's telling the truth and he spent the night alone. If he hadn't, why would he have left the hotel so early? He must have been out of there by 7.30 a.m. to be back by now. But perhaps whoever he'd been with hadn't stayed overnight, Natalie tells herself. Perhaps she has a family too; she might have needed to get home. And Kara was back last night, wasn't she? Maybe he and Kara decided to stagger their arrival times home, so as not to arouse suspicion.

Jake comes into the living room, holding a damp and forlorn-looking Loulou at arm's length. 'I just found it in the lanes. What was it doing out there?'

Natalie feels panic race through her. Last night when she went into Elsie's room, she didn't notice the doll was gone, though why would she have noticed such an innocuous detail when her own child was missing? Elsie must have taken it with her when she wandered out of the house. But how is she supposed to explain this to Jake?

'Oh, thank goodness,' she says, taking the doll from him. 'We've been looking for her everywhere.' She squeezes the doll's soft leg and feels the cold seep into her fingers. Jake is looking at her questioningly, waiting for an explanation. 'We went for a walk. Yesterday.'

'So she's been out there all night. You managed to get Elsie to sleep without it?'

Neither of them is ever likely to forget the last night Loulou wasn't there at bedtime. They'd scoured the house from top to bottom, as Natalie did hours earlier, until Elsie's distress became so intense that Jake was forced to take his search outside, where Loulou was eventually found abandoned in one of the barns. As soon as the doll was in her arms, Elsie had fallen into a deep and immediate sleep, exhausted by her melt-down. No wonder he seems sceptical now when she tries to suggest that all was fine without it.

Natalie shrugs. 'Somehow. Maybe it's a phase she's growing out of. You know how quickly kids move from one thing to the next.'

Jake's eyes narrow. Natalie knows it's not a convincing lie: Elsie has been attached to that doll for nearly two years.

'So how did it go?'

'How did what go?'

'The ice cream,' Natalie says, wondering why she needs to remind him of the purpose of his trip to Bristol. She already knows the trip wasn't a success. If it had been, she surely would have heard about it as soon as Jake had stepped foot through the front door.

'Oh. It was a no. Sorry... I tried my best.'

'Who was there?'

'Where?'

'At the pitch,' she says slowly, finding herself grow irritable. 'Who was there?'

His mouth turns upwards, lips thinning as he contemplates her interest in details that to him must now seem unnecessary. 'A man and a woman. Both older than us. Company executives.'

'What was she wearing?'

'What?'

She realises the ridiculousness of the question, but she can't help herself. If Jake isn't lying, the answer should come quickly enough to him. The truth shouldn't need consideration in the way a lie will. 'I don't know,' he snaps. 'A black dress, I think. He was wearing grey. Both nondescript... what is this, Natalie?'

She sighs as she considers her own paranoia. This isn't the woman she wants to be.

'I'm sorry about the ice cream,' he says, going to her and putting his arms around her. 'It would have taken some pressure off, and I know how much it means to you. But it's the first sales pitch we've tried. Maybe it was my fault; maybe I didn't pitch it hard enough. I'll do it differently next time.'

'It's not your fault.'

She feels herself flinch beneath his embrace, as he too has flinched from any physical contact she's tried to initiate. Why is he doing this now, after being away from home all night? They seem to Natalie the attentions of a guilty man.

'There'll be others. We'll keep going now, okay?'

They are interrupted by Natalie's phone; she answers the call as she takes Loulou upstairs to Elsie.

'Hello, Mrs Prosser? This is Dr Lynch from the surgery.'

Elsie's blood test results. Natalie knows there's something wrong. If the results are clear, it's always a receptionist who calls with them.

'We've got the results of Elsie's blood test,' Dr Lynch confirms. 'I'm sorry they've taken so long to come back. There was tetracycline found in her sample.'

'Tetracycline,' Natalie repeats. 'What's that?'

'It's a type of antibiotic. But it's not prescribed to young children because of the side effects. It's very likely to be the cause of Elsie's lethargy and sickness. It can also cause intracranial hypertension, so I'd like to get Elsie booked in for a CT scan.'

The words surround Natalie like a fog as she stops on the landing. 'Intracranial hypertension. What is that?'

'Pressure around the brain. Mrs Prosser, we know that Elsie didn't get a prescription from this surgery, so we need to know how she came to ingest this medication.'

Natalie tastes vomit in her mouth. She has no idea how this

could have happened, or where the medication might have come from. Elsie is in recovery; her little body shouldn't have to contend with anything more. And what if it's not able to?

Social services are going to be involved. Perhaps Elsie will be taken away from them.

'I don't know,' she says, panicked. 'There's nothing like that in the house. The only medications here are the ones prescribed to me and they're all kept out of reach in the bathroom cupboard – there's no way Elsie can get her hands on them.'

'It will help if we can identify the medication Elsie took, as well as being able to work out how much she may have consumed.'

Tears prick at Natalie's eyes. Clutching the phone, she goes to her daughter's bedroom, where Elsie's still playing with her doll's house. Her beautiful little girl. She would never do anything to harm her. She would never let anyone or anything hurt her.

And yet last night she left the house unsecured. Something terrible might have happened. And now this.

The cattle, she thinks, the thought pinging into her head like a snapshot memory of a nightmare. The cow was given antibiotics.

She puts the doctor on loudspeaker as she accesses the internet on her phone. She whispers to Elsie that Daddy is home, and watches her daughter rush out to see him. She types Tetracycline into the search engine, along with the word cattle. Used for bacterial infections, the results immediately tell her. Can cause sickness, diarrhoea and lethargy in young children.

'I need to speak to my husband,' she says quietly.

The call is ended, but she knows it's just a matter of time before they get a knock at the front door. Natalie goes downstairs to speak to Jake. A terrifying thought passes over her, halting her in her tracks. What if this was no accident? Jake was responsible for the cow's antibiotics. What if he knew Elsie had got her hands on that medication?

She goes to the living room, where Jake and Elsie are sitting together on the sofa. When she looks at him, she realises she doesn't recognise him as the husband she loves. Can she trust this man? she wonders. She hates that the question has even crossed her mind. He's the father of her child; her best friend. It shouldn't occur to her that he might, after all, not be what he seems. And yet the feeling has taken hold of her and snared her with a strength she hadn't anticipated, refusing to be shaken off.

She opens her mouth to mention the antibiotics, but doubt keeps the words trapped.

'Where did you find it?' Jake says.

'Find what?'

He points to the blue pot she returned earlier to its rightful place on the mantelpiece.

'Oh. It was on my bedside table. I never put it there though. Someone else must have moved it.'

Jake's eyes narrow. 'Who?' he says, making no attempt to hide the scepticism in his voice. His tone tells her all she needs to know: he still thinks she's responsible for moving it, that she's somehow managed to forget doing so. She doesn't get a chance to answer. As she goes to speak, Kara appears in the doorway.

'How did the trip go?' she asks.

'A no-go, I'm afraid. But a useful experience. We'll have better luck next time, I'm sure.'

'I'm sure you will.' Kara looks from Jake to Natalie, her eyes resting on her for a moment too long.

'Are you okay?' Jake asks Natalie. 'You don't look too well.'

'I'm fine. I think I'll just go for a lie down.'

Natalie doesn't care now whether the two of them are left alone. If something's going on, it's going to happen, whatever she does. But she won't trust either of them with Elsie, knowing what she does now. She looks at the doll sitting beside Elsie on the sofa and feels sick at the thought of Jake knowingly harming their daughter.

'Elsie,' she says quickly. 'Come upstairs please.'

'I've only just got back,' Jake begins to object.

'She needs to get dressed.'

Natalie takes Elsie by the arm. She feels Jake and Kara both staring at her, watching her seemingly erratic behaviour. She sweeps her daughter up into her arms and glances past Kara as she makes her way to the staircase.

She reaches out and grabs Natalie's arm. 'Don't worry,' she says with a smile. 'I won't say anything about last night.'

TWENTY

When I go to look for Jake late on Monday afternoon I see Natalie entering one of the barns, also looking for him. Her phone is gripped in her hand and her face is wet with tears. She hasn't seen me, so I wait at the side of the barn, ready to tell them I need Natalie's help with something in the house if either of them sees me here. Their conversation quickly escalates into a heated argument.

'Where did you keep the antibiotics you were giving the cow?' she asks him.

'In one of the barns. Why?'

'Elsie's blood test results came back. She's taken those antibiotics somehow. There was tetracycline in her system. The doctor said that's probably what's been causing her sickness and tiredness. She wants her to have a CT scan.'

'When did you find this out?'

'A few days ago.'

'And you're only now telling me? Why didn't you tell me when you found out?'

Natalie takes a deep breath. She doesn't want to admit that

she suspected him. 'Is that really the issue here? How did she get her hands on them, Jake?'

'I don't know. She couldn't have – they've been kept up on a shelf.'

'But she's taken them. It must have been those; it can't possibly be anything else. How could you be so careless?'

'This is my fault?'

'Well, who else's would it be?'

This is perfect. This is exactly how things fall apart, because the wider the gap between them becomes, the easier it will be to break them. They don't trust each other, and without it they have nothing.

'Social services have just called me,' Natalie says, her voice cracking on every word. 'The surgery must have contacted them. They're coming here tomorrow morning.'

'Why?'

'They'll want to talk to us about how this could have happened. They'll be checking to see whether the farm's a safe enough place for Elsie. What if they take her away from us?'

'They can't do that. They'd need to have evidence and—'

'What more evidence do they need? The medication was picked up in a blood test. The vet will confirm the prescription for the cow. They won't need to prove anything, it's all here waiting for them.'

'Did the doctor say whether they're going to give anything to treat Elsie?' Jake asks. 'Will there be any long-term side effects?'

'I don't know. The scan will tell us more. How could you let this happen?'

I wait for Jake to defend himself, but he doesn't. A moment later, shaking and still visibly upset, Natalie comes storming from the barn. She heads back to the house and, once I've seen her gone, I go into the barn to console Jake.

'What have you just heard?' he asks me.

'When? Nothing. I've just come from the house.'

He eyes me warily, unsure if I'm telling the truth. I try to kiss him, but he doesn't let me. When I go back to the house, Natalie's sitting on the sofa with a blanket over her, though her face is flushed and she looks as though she's running a temperature. I offer to do bedtime with Elsie.

'Thank you,' she says, little gratitude in her blunt tone. 'But I'll do it.'

'You always do it. You rarely get a night off.'

'She's used to me doing it. She won't even let Jake do bedtimes.'

'Exactly. You never get a break.'

'What happened on Friday—' she begins.

'—is forgotten about,' I say, finishing her sentence. 'I won't say a word about anything, I promise. Let me do bedtime. You need the rest.'

She protests again, and I don't argue any further, letting her think she's won. I leave her alone in the living room, and when I come back twenty minutes later she's fallen asleep, the medication I slipped in her tea earlier having worked its magic. When I go upstairs, Elsie is in her bedroom, playing with her dolls. They sit propped against the doll's house, legs splayed to keep them upright.

'What are you playing?'

'School.'

'Is one of them you?'

She points to a doll with blonde hair. 'Mummy,' she says, picking up another, this time brunette.

'Oh, Mummy's there too. Is it the start of school, or is she picking you up?'

Elsie says nothing. She's ignorant to the point of being rude at times, and her speech is annoyingly babyish.

'Shall I tell you a story?' I say, picking up a doll with red hair. 'It's about a little girl who goes to school one day. Her mummy drops her off, like this—' I walk the doll to the door of the house '—but at home time there's a surprise. Do you want to know what it is?'

I'm not convinced she does. Elsie's face is scrunched, her eyes watching mine beneath a tangle of curls. She says nothing, but she's still listening.

'Her mummy isn't there. Her daddy picks her up from school and when they get home, Mummy isn't there either. She's disappeared.'

Elsie scowls. 'I don't like.'

I put a hand on her back and rub it gently in a circular motion, telling myself all the while that I can do this. It might not come naturally, but it will come, eventually.

'I know. No one likes it when it happens. But sometimes it does happen. Being a mummy is a very hard job. Some people aren't good at it. They get too tired, you see.'

I notice Elsie squirming and reaching between her legs.

'Do you need a wee?'

She shakes her head vehemently.

'Okay. Tell me if you do though, okay.'

Elsie looks at the brunette doll still in her hand and turns it around as though assessing it. 'Mummy was poorly.'

'Yes, she was. And she's still poorly; that's why we need to look after her. But sometimes people don't get better, you know that, don't you? Does Mummy ever talk to you about your nanny and bampy?'

Elsie shifts away from me on the carpet. 'In Heaven,' she says, eyeing me warily.

'That's right... in Heaven. They're all happy there. Mummy might have to go there soon too, to see them. She'll be okay there; they'll look after her.'

Elsie's face changes; she looks as though she's about to cry. When I look down, I realise why she's got upset. Her pink leggings are stained dark where she's wet herself. 'For God's sake, Elsie, I asked if you needed a wee!'

I grab her by the arm and yank her up from the carpet. She starts crying loudly now, telling me I'm hurting her.

'Stop,' I say, desperate to quieten her and not rouse Natalie. 'Please, Elsie. I'm sorry, okay. I'm sorry.'

But it's too late. Elsie rushes past me and runs downstairs to Natalie, calling out to her. I quickly follow, finding Elsie lying on top of her mother in the living room, sobbing into the blankets.

'I'm sorry—' I start to apologise.

'What's happened?' Natalie says quickly, shaking herself awake and eyeing me as though I'm some kind of monster. 'It's okay,' she says soothingly into Elsie's hair. 'You're okay now. It's just an accident.' She lifts Elsie's face to kiss her forehead, but the girl won't be pacified. If Natalie realises she seems more upset than normal she does nothing to question it.

'Was she in her bed?'

'No. On the carpet.'

'I'll come up and deal with it now. You should have woken me.'

She eases Elsie off her and stands from the sofa, carrying her piss-stained daughter into the hallway.

I watch them head upstairs before I go into the living room. The television is on, its sound turned down, and now I worry how much Natalie may have heard. I wonder whether she was still asleep when Elsie came down here, or whether she'd already woken and was listening on the landing. The house is old and the floorboards creak, though; I'm certain I would have heard her if she'd come upstairs.

But what if I didn't?

I thought I could do this – I thought I could take Elsie on and be a parent to her alongside Jake. I'd imagined the three of us, happy in our new set-up: Jake a little more in love with me for accepting Elsie as though my own; Elsie happy in her new life. Me, faking it until I made it. But I can't. I never asked for a package deal. I don't want a boil-in-the-bag, ready-made family. I don't want a child in my life. I just want Jake. He's all I've ever wanted. Somehow, Natalie and Elsie both need to disappear.

TWENTY-ONE

Natalie wakes even earlier than usual on Tuesday morning, worry having kept her awake for most of the night. By 5 a.m. she's out in the barns feeding the cattle, and when she returns to the house she sets about tidying the living room and cleaning the bathroom and kitchen as quietly as she can, not wanting to rouse Elsie from her sleep. The last thing they need is for her to be tired and grumpy when the social worker arrives.

'You can't stay in those,' Natalie says, when Jake comes into the kitchen, casting a disapproving glance at his dirty work clothes. 'Go and get changed. She could be here any minute.'

When Elsie wakes she dresses her in a pinafore dress and tights, making sure her hair's neatly brushed. 'A lady's coming to see us today,' she tells her, but Elsie says nothing in response. 'She might ask you some questions. Just tell her the truth, okay? She just wants to know that you're happy.'

Natalie's eyes fill with tears as she studies her daughter's innocent face. A swell of guilt rises in her chest. She may not have put those antibiotics in front of her, but it feels as though she might as well have done. They're going to take her away, she thinks, and before she can stop them, fat tears stain her cheeks.

'Mama,' Elsie says, her little voice etched with concern.

'I'm fine,' Natalie says, wiping her eyes with the sleeve of her sweater. 'They're just happy tears.'

She goes to get changed, and at 10 a.m. the doorbell rings. Jake stands at the living room doorway, looking more presentable now in jeans and a shirt. They're met with a woman in her late forties who introduces herself as Caroline and accepts an offer of tea, doing nothing to hide her assessment of the farmhouse while she waits with Natalie when Jake goes to the kitchen to put the kettle on.

'And you must be Elsie,' she says, pulling her attention from the house. 'What a pretty dress.'

Elsie says nothing. Natalie hopes she won't maintain this silent act for the duration of the social worker's visit. It's only going to make things look even worse.

'Do you go to nursery, Elsie?'

Elsie nods.

'And do you know what it's called?'

'She goes to The Meadows day nursery,' Natalie volunteers, when Elsie doesn't offer a response.

'How many days a week?'

'Just three mornings.'

Caroline nods. She takes something from her bag and hands it to Elsie. It's a small colouring book with a pack of crayons attached. 'Here,' she says, taking the book back so she can open the packet of crayons. 'Would you like to do one of these for me now?'

Elsie takes the book and crayons and sits on the rug at the coffee table, busily occupying herself with her task while Caroline starts a series of questions about the referral from the surgery.

'I understand Elsie took some antibiotics that weren't meant for her.'

Natalie nods, shamed by the fact.

'Do you know how many she might have taken?'

'No. I don't know how she managed to get them. They were kept in one of the barns, up on a shelf. Jake can show you when he comes back.'

Caroline studies her with the kind of sympathetic look Natalie hates to be on the receiving end of. 'And how are things for you at the moment?'

'Fine.'

'The doctor tells me you may be under some pressure... that you were taken to hospital recently.'

'I fainted and banged my head,' Natalie says defensively, wondering why the doctor is sharing details of her medical history. 'I was only kept overnight as a precaution.'

She's grateful when Jake comes back into the room. He hands them both a cup of tea. 'Everything okay?'

'Natalie tells me you'll be able to show me where these antibiotics were kept.'

'Of course,' Jake says, casting Natalie a glance. 'The cow they were prescribed for has finished the course now, so they're all gone, but I'll show you where we keep everything else.'

As she passes, Caroline puts a hand on Natalie's arm. 'I just want to make sure everything's safe. That's all.'

Natalie stays with Elsie while Jake and Caroline go outside. The wait for their return feels longer than she knows it probably is, but in those minutes there's too much quiet for her mind not to take her to all the places she doesn't want to go. What if the social worker somehow finds out about what happened a few nights ago? They'll think her completely unfit to take care of her own daughter. The woman's already questioning her state of mind; she could see it in her eyes when she asked about her hospital visit.

By the time they return, Elsie's grown bored of colouring and has gone up to her bedroom to play with her toys. Caroline talks them through home safety, reminding them of things

Natalie already knows. She asks questions about Elsie's eating and her sleep patterns.

'I'm satisfied that this was an accident, and that the necessary measures have been put in place to make sure nothing like this happens again,' she eventually tells them, after what to Natalie have felt like the longest hours of her life.

She feels herself sag with relief. 'Thank you.'

'So what happens next?' Jake asks.

'Nothing. I'll sign the matter off and you won't be hearing from me again.'

They see her out of the house together, and after watching her car pull off the driveway, Natalie feels panic sweep over her. 'She must think one of us drugged her.'

'She just said she was signing us off,' Jake says, bewildered. 'She wouldn't be doing that if she thought Elsie had been drugged intentionally.'

'But what if she's just saying that? What if she doesn't believe us, and she's lulling us into a false sense of security? She might come back here, unannounced.'

'You're being irrational. I don't think they can do that.'

'Have you ever had involvement with social services before?' she snaps at him. 'Neither of us has any idea how they might operate.'

'I'm not doing this.' Jake turns to walk away, and Natalie feels a surge of resentment rise in her stomach, making her feel sick.

'You must have left those pills lying around somewhere,' she pleads. 'Think. Please. If you can remember where it might have happened, we can stop this going any further. People make mistakes. They might forgive us an error, but they're not going to let it go if they think this was done on purpose.'

'She's not taking it any further!' The words burst from him, his face reddening. 'What do you want me to do, Natalie – admit that I gave them to Elsie myself? I didn't leave them lying around, and I don't know how she managed to take them. She's just said nothing more is going to happen. How many times do you need to hear something before you fucking listen?'

He leaves the hallway, and in the silence that follows Natalie thinks her heart might burst from her chest. She has never seen him so angry, and she can't remember him ever speaking to her like this before.

She feels the panic attack come on: she's had them before, several over the years, always catching her off-guard. Her breathing becomes shallow and her chest tightens; she tries to swallow gulps of air but it feels as though her throat's constricted and nothing can get past. Panicked, she leaves the living room and goes to the front door, desperate for a burst of fresh air.

It's started raining. The drops feel cool on her skin and she wanders out onto the driveway, around the house towards the start of the fields, still desperately trying to fill her lungs. The pigsty lies ahead of her, both animals inside, sheltered from the cold. A part of her knows she's being irrational, but her mind won't allow her to focus. They're on social service's radar now. Anything they do or don't do may come back to haunt them. She stands at the fence, hands pressed to the wood as the breath begins to come back to her, and when she turns back to the house, she sees a figure at the landing window: Kara, just standing there, watching her.

TWENTY-TWO

I go out to Natalie, who is standing at the fence that surrounds the pigsty. She's staring blankly at the churned up mud. I put a hand on her arm, and she flinches beneath my touch.

'Are you okay?'

'Fine.'

She won't want me to know the details of whatever the social worker's said. I saw the woman go outside with Jake to the barns. Though I've no idea what was concluded before the woman left, I assume they won't let the matter drop now, not while both Jake and Natalie will be denying knowing how Elsie might have got her hands on that medication.

But I can't say anything to her about it. I'm not supposed to know what's been going on.

'You look pale,' I say gently. 'Come back to the house, I'll make you a cup of tea.'

'I said I'm fine. Thank you.' When I glance at Natalie, her eyes are filled with tears. She's coming apart, her life unravelling around her. Yet still she attempts to remain stoic, putting on the kind of brave face that's capable of fooling no one.

'I've just seen Jake,' I tell her. 'He looked upset. Has something happened?'

She turns sharply to me, her face darkened. 'Nothing's happened. Everything's fine.'

She turns and heads back to the house, and a while later I see her take Elsie out in the car. When I find Jake in one of the barns, he's similarly aloof.

'Who was that woman I saw you with earlier?'

'A nurse. Here about Elsie... you know, just a check-up.'

I never thought Jake would lie to me, yet he manages it so easily. I go to him and put a hand on his neck, but he pushes it away.

'Not now. Please.'

The rejection burns. 'I'm just trying to help.'

'You're not helping anything,' he snaps.

Something I've suspected for too long already now is cemented in this moment. We are not a team. Despite what I've managed to convince myself of for so long now, we never really have been. He shuts me out when it suits him to; he picks me up again when he's ready.

'Is something going on with Elsie? Is she okay?'

'For fuck's sake, I've just told you everything is fine.'

'Same as Natalie said. But you're both liars.'

He grabs me by the shoulders. 'Just leave her alone. Stop fucking poking your nose in all the time.'

He looks as though he's either about to hit me or start crying, so I do the thing that comes instinctively to me and put a hand to the back of his head, pulling him towards me and kissing him. He responds at first, his tongue finding mine. Then he pulls away, repelled, and shoves me with both hands, sending me flailing backwards. I trip as I stumble, and my head hits the metal rail of the cattle enclosure. Jake looks at me, stunned by what's just happened.

'I'm sorry,' he says, offering a hand to help me up. 'I didn't mean—'

'Forget it.' I get myself up, putting a hand to the back of my head, feeling the lump that's already started to form there. 'I get the message.'

He calls me back as I leave the barn, but I ignore him and return to the farmhouse, my chest burning with anger. He's never laid a hand on me like that before. I get my laptop and take it to the kitchen, where I run an internet search on local social services, finding the contact details for the department that deals with child protection concerns. I quickly set up a new email account, using a false name.

To whom it may concern, I begin. I have concerns for a local child who I believe may be at risk of neglect: Elsie Prosser, who lives with her parents on Llanafon Dairy Farm. I live in the village, and late last week, while driving home late from a work event, I passed the child on one of the rural lanes about half a mile from the farm. This was around 2.30 a.m. Elsie was wearing pyjamas and was being carried by a woman who I know not to be her mother. The woman was carrying her back to the farm, so I can only assume that Elsie had been somehow able to leave her home without her parents' knowledge. She was lucky that the woman was there to help her. It raises serious questions about the security of the farm and Elsie's welfare. As this is a small community, I would prefer to remain anonymous.

It implicates them both, something I've never intended to do before now. But when they're asked about that night, Jake will be able to tell them he was away. He'll have proof of his hotel booking, and the hotel will be able to confirm he was there all night. Everything will come back to Natalie. Negligent. Irresponsible. An unfit mother.

I run my hand over the back of my head, my fingertips finding the smooth lump that's risen beneath my hair. Perhaps

Jake should be implicated anyway. He's volatile. Violent. Maybe they'll both be investigated, and maybe now, after all the lies and the empty promises, I actually no longer care what happens to him.

TWENTY-THREE

On Wednesday Kara goes for a run. She does this three times a week, usually on the same mornings, and the predictability of her pattern allows Natalie a window of opportunity that she has been thinking about for the past few days since Jake's trip to Bristol. She knows Jake is being unfaithful. And she knows someone gave Elsie those antibiotics intentionally. She'd seen Kara at the barns that evening; she could have lied about having been for a run. Natalie just doesn't want to believe for a moment that Jake may be involved. But so much has happened in those past few weeks, so much that has sent her mind and her sanity reeling. Jake and Kara could have been working together, and the more she turns the possibility in her mind, the more plausible it becomes.

Elsie's still in bed, and when Natalie goes into her room to check on her she looks at her daughter and wonders at how perfect she is. She seems so small lying on her single mattress, the transition from toddler to 'big girl' bed a recent one. She pictures Elsie as she saw her a few months earlier, pale and grey beneath a thin hospital blanket, the small foot protruding from the rough grey-white cotton jabbed with a cannula that had taken an eventually flustered doctor and two nurses four attempts to insert, Elsie had put up such a fight.

The same doctor, calmed now, would later praise Natalie for acting so quickly in response to her daughter's symptoms. At the doctor's surgery – and later again at the hospital – professionals had misdiagnosed her with a viral infection, the temperature and lethargy the symptoms of a whole host of common childhood illnesses. The rash had come on day three, pink and mottled in an angry spread across her lower back, and, when Natalie had taken her to A&E fearing meningitis, the doctors had admitted to uncertainty about what was causing Elsie's condition.

The doctor wouldn't be praising her if he could see them now, Natalie thinks. Guilt rises in her gut like bile. The image of Elsie prone in the hospital bed is replaced with another: Elsie in her princess pyjamas in Kara's arms, tiny and vulnerable in the cold of the night. Elsie throwing up over a café floor, poisoned with medication meant for the cattle. Natalie closes her eyes as she wills away the images. She has to find out what's happening.

Natalie has never been into Kara's bedroom. From the day she moved in, the room became Kara's domain, the only space in the house exclusively hers. It would never have occurred to Natalie to go in there. Now, it feels like a necessity. She stops for a moment at the bedroom door, her palm poised at the handle. This is Jake. They have been together since they were fourteen years old, and in over thirteen years spent with each other they have been through more than some couples twice their age. They have suffered loss together, grieved together, run a business as a couple, brought a child into the world. Their entire adult lives thus far have been navigated around one another.

But time changes people, she thinks. Just how much has it

changed Jake? Enough that he'd harm his own daughter to appease his lover?

She pushes down the handle and enters the bedroom. Kara's made her mark on the place, trying to soften it with throws and cushions. She stops by the side of the bed and studies it unblinkingly, her heart pausing for a moment at the thought that perhaps Jake has been here, with her. She fights away an involuntary image, his naked limbs tangled with Kara's, and, as she swallows down a rush of self-pity, she calms herself with a reminder of why she is here.

On the bedside table near the window there's a phone charger and a paperback titled *Living with Less: A Guide to Leading a Simpler Life*. Natalie thumbs through the pages, catching snippets of advice on decluttering and chapter headings such as 'The Friendship Detox'. She wonders what the author's opinion on seducing other people's husbands would be. She closes the book and opens the top drawer of the bedside table, finding nothing but a blank notebook, a few pens and a packet of jelly babies. In the next drawer down there are underwear and socks, and in the third drawer a kindle and a selection of charging leads.

She opens the wardrobe, unsurprised now by the limited number of clothes Kara owns. At some point, whether since moving here or earlier, Kara has apparently been minimalising her life, and Natalie can't help but wonder why. Kara comes from a life that remains a mystery to them, and Natalie realises she has created a fantasy existence for her, seeped in glamour and excitement, probably a million miles from the life that had really been hers. It occurs to her now that in building this exotic background for a woman who is little more than a stranger to her, Natalie's really been crafting a fantasy for herself, one that allows her to momentarily escape from the monotony and worry of her own daily life.

In the bottom of the wardrobe are piles of towels and bedding, of which there are more than Kara's clothes. Natalie moves some aside and finds, concealed beneath them, two plastic boxes with clip-shut lids. She slides out the first: when she opens it she wishes she hadn't. Inside is a collection of lingerie: soft cottons, lace; beneath them, PVC. She pulls out something she suspects is a thong but could be anything from a slingshot to a choker; she's unsure where it's supposed to go or how it's meant to stay in place. Her pulse quickens. As far as she knows, Kara doesn't have a boyfriend and hasn't been seeing anyone. *As far as she knows*. Perhaps that's the point: she isn't supposed to know.

Not really wanting to see what's inside the second but aware her curiosity will haunt her for not looking, she removes the lid. Immediately she recoils from the sight of what she finds. She's never considered herself a prude, but perhaps that's what she is, she thinks. Maybe this is why Jake's been tempted to stray, and why wouldn't he, when there's apparently so much more of interest on offer elsewhere? The box is filled with rubber and plastic sex toys, all shapes, sizes and colours. It occurs to her as she reluctantly peers closer among the items that she's incredibly naïve: she's no idea what half these things are for, where they go or what their intended purpose is.

She slams the lid back on the box. She feels sick. Jake hasn't gone near her in months, and for months she's blamed herself for his absence, chiding herself for letting herself go, for not having more energy; for simply not being enough. Every time she's tried to touch him he's flinched from her as though he finds her repulsive. Natalie closes her eyes and fights back the urge to hurl the box across the room. This isn't her. It's not who she is. But who is she, really? She's not sure she knows any more.

She puts the boxes back in the wardrobe and covers them as she found them. When she goes to the window, she sees Kara running along the length of lane that edges the side boundary of the farmland, heading back to the house. She's wearing the blue hoodie. Her long hair bounces in a high ponytail as her trainers hit the tarmac. Even running, she manages to look beautiful.

If her aim in giving Elsie those antibiotics was to make Natalie look like a bad mother, she's got what she wanted. But she's also implicated Jake; he's as responsible for Elsie's welfare as she is, and he's the one accountable for the cattle's medications. Kara must have known that would happen. Whatever their relationship is, she can't possibly love him if she's willing to throw him under the bus in a way so he'd be in danger of losing his own child.

With a thundering heart, Natalie leaves the bedroom and goes to her own, where she sits on the end of the bed and waits to hear the front door. She can't confront Kara. She'd rather speak with Jake first, although she suspects if she was to ask him for the truth he wouldn't give it to her. Her fingers grip the edge of the bed as she focuses on her breathing. She's had her life ripped from beneath her once before. She knows what it is to have the foundations of her world burned and reduced to ash. One thing remained despite everything: she survived it. But she isn't sure whether she's strong enough to get through it again.

TWENTY-FOUR

As soon as Natalie leaves the house to take Elsie to the leisure centre, I corner Jake in the kitchen. We've barely had a chance to talk since he pushed me over in the barn; we've managed to keep our exchanges brief, neither addressing the subject of what happened.

'Can we talk?'

'About what?'

'You know what.'

He glances at the kitchen window, checking the driveway. Natalie's car hasn't yet left the drive, but it sometimes takes her an age to get Elsie into her car seat.

'I said I was sorry for what happened. I should never have pushed you like that.'

'Sorry isn't enough.'

'I'll make it up to you, I promise.'

'How?'

'Whatever it takes. But please, we can't do this now.'

'Then when?'

We hear the sound of the front door, and Jake quickly heads

to the porch where he feigns taking off his wellies. I'm at the sink when Natalie comes in.

'That was a quick swim,' I say casually.

'Forgot Elsie's armbands,' she says, rolling her eyes. She goes to a bag that's been left hanging on one of the dining chairs and fumbles in it before producing them like a magician pulling a rabbit from a hat. 'I'll do the shopping on the way back,' she tells Jake.

She goes back to the hallway, but I notice her pause before she gets to the front door. I don't believe her story. I think she forgot the armbands on purpose, so she'd have a reason to come back here. She's suspicious of everyone at the moment, constantly watching everything that's going on in the house. Her nerves must be on edge waiting for a knock at the door from social services.

'See you later,' she calls out, too cheerfully. I watch at the kitchen window, waiting here to see her car leave the driveway. In the porch, Jake takes his wellies back off. I'd expected him to scarper off to the barns as soon as he had a chance, but apparently he wants to stay.

'I'm sorry about what happened,' he says.

'You already said that.'

'I'd never do anything to hurt you.'

'That's not true though, is it? This *is* hurting me. Every day I wake up knowing you're still with her. I'm just left hanging on to the hope of us being together – one day. But that day never seems to come. That's hurting me.'

'We just need to wait until all this crap with social services is over.'

'But there's always something, isn't there? There was another excuse before that, and there'll be another one after it. If you don't want me any more, I'd rather you just say.'

'Of course I want you.'

'Then prove it.'

I kiss him. He hesitates, still on edge though we know that Natalie's gone. I pull him against me and kiss him again, harder this time, feeling his body against mine finally relenting.

'Come upstairs with me,' I say. 'Natalie will be gone a couple of hours, at least.'

'I can't.'

But I feel him growing hard against me, his erection pressed against my hip. His cold hands trace my waist, reaching under my T-shirt and finding the dips in the flesh that curve towards my groin. I hear my own sharp intake of breath as clearly as he must, and when I pull back from him and take his hand in mine he follows me now without objection. We go upstairs to the bedroom. He clicks the door shut behind us and then his hands move beneath my T-shirt again, his rough fingertips scanning my skin. They find the flat of my stomach, my waist, my chest.

We remove each other's clothes with the urgency that was once second nature to us when we first starting sleeping together. I know every contour of his body, every scar and imperfection; I know him better than anyone ever has or ever will.

'I love you,' I tell him.

'I love you too.' He runs his hands through my hair, his fingers finding the lump on the back of my head. 'I am so, so sorry,' he says, kissing my scalp, his lips moving across my ear to find my face. 'I'll make everything up to you, I promise.'

He pushes me onto the bed and covers my body with his, his mouth exploring my chest and my stomach, working his way down. We are so distracted with each other, so busy making up for all the lost time, that neither of us hears anyone at the door, so when it bursts open we are both exposed, both naked on top of the duvet. Jake lunges to the floor for his T-shirt before holding it against his torso as though it might in some way undo what's already been witnessed. She looks at him blankly, shock fixed on her face before it's replaced with an expression of disgust. She holds his eye for an uncomfortable period of time, the three of us submerged in a silence that feels so heavy it might drown us. Then she looks over to me, disapproval twisting her mouth into a grimace.

Eventually, Jake breaks the silence, his voice little more than a whisper. 'Tyler,' he says without looking at me. 'Put some clothes on.' And then he looks back at her, his expression desperate. 'Kara. I can explain.'

PART TWO

TWENTY-FIVE

My eyes rest on Kara and the look of shock on her face. She must have come here knowing what she was going to find, though. Natalie is out with Elsie; there's only the three of us here. So how long ago did she work it out? She doesn't want to have to look at either of us, but like an eyewitness to a traffic collision, she can't bring herself to look away from the chaos. There's a moment of stifling silence in which nobody moves, the three of us absorbing the stupidity of Jake's words. *I can explain.* I'd love to know how he plans to go about it.

Jake edges to the side of the bed and reaches to the carpet for the rest of his clothes. 'This isn't what it looks like.'

I wish he would stop talking. I grab my sweater from the floor and wriggle awkwardly back into my trousers. Kara takes a sneak peek, trying to make out she hasn't. Dressed now, Jake sits on the edge of the bed, head lowered like a child awaiting a telling-off. The brazen bitch holds my eye, too defiant to look away. She thinks she isn't scared of me. That'll soon change.

'Why did you come in here?' I ask.

'Am I really the one who needs to explain myself?' She turns her attention to Jake. The stupid bear she's holding stares at me blank-eyed. 'I'm assuming Natalie doesn't know about this.' Her voice is thick with sarcasm and a disdain so heavy it thickens the air in the room.

Jake shakes his head. He's dressed himself so hurriedly his shirt is buttoned up wrong.

'Please,' he says, his voice irritatingly pathetic. 'Don't tell her.'

'Then you're going to have to. Natalie's been good to me. I don't want to see her made a fool of.'

'That's not what I'm doing, Kara. Please. It's complicated.'

I wish he'd stop begging. He sounds desperate.

'How long has this been going on?'

'That's a conversation for my wife,' Jake says, at last showing a bit of fire.

'Then have it,' Kara snipes back. 'Tell her, or I will.'

She looks back at me with disgust before turning and leaving the room, slamming the door on her way out.

'Fuck,' Jake says. 'Fuck, fuck, fuck.'

I sit beside him and put a hand on his knee. 'Stop panicking. She won't say anything. Where's she going to go if she does?'

Jake looks unconvinced. 'It won't be hard for her to find somewhere else. And they've become friends. She'll tell her everything.'

I shake my head. 'I don't think they're that close. Natalie seems to have been avoiding her recently, if anything. Let me talk to her.'

He eyes me suspiciously. 'What are you going to do?'

'Talk to her,' I repeat. 'That's all. Stay here.'

I go downstairs to the kitchen, where I find Kara standing at the sink drinking a glass of water.

'Why did you come into the bedroom?'

She drains the glass before putting it in the sink. 'I've seen the way you look at him. Like you said, Natalie's out. I heard two people in there, and I knew it could only have been you.'

'And you wanted to see for yourself?'

She says nothing, but she gives me that look of hers: the same look she gave me the day she moved in here, when I'd carried her bags upstairs for her. She thinks she knows what's going on here; she thinks herself so clever to have worked it all out. But she knows nothing. No one knows this family like I do. She doesn't belong here. I do.

'You're not going to say a word to Natalie.'

'Says who?'

'Let me tell you something about this place, Kara. It's a dangerous business, farming. Accidents can happen easily, anywhere. You're a city girl, aren't you? You're not equipped for this life. I'd get out while you still can.'

'Are you threatening me?'

'Call it a friendly warning.'

She's trying to act as though she isn't scared, but I can see the fear in her eyes. She won't say a word, not by the time I'm finished with her. There's nothing for her here; she doesn't have anything to lose by leaving. She and Natalie aren't friends: they barely know each other. This place is everything to me. Jake, the farm... I've waited too long for them to have a stranger take it all away.

'Natalie talks about you like a brother,' Kara says. 'How can you do this to her?'

'You don't know anything about us. You don't belong here.'

I step closer to her, and she flinches. I see her search the worktops for something to grab, but there's nothing available. I'm not going to hurt her, anyway. Not yet.

'Go and pack your things,' I tell her. 'Don't speak to Jake. Don't leave anything for Natalie. Don't contact her again, okay? If you do, I'll know about it.'

'I see what you are, Tyler. Natalie may be blind to it, but you've never fooled me.'

I lower my face to hers, so close that when I speak my breath hits her face. 'Why are you still here?'

Finally doing what's best for her, she leaves and goes upstairs. It shouldn't take long for her to pack her things; she came with next to nothing. Her sad little life amounts to a suitcase and a few boxes. Jake comes downstairs after hearing Kara go into her bedroom. He looks grey with worry.

'What are we going to do?'

I put a hand to his face and kiss him. 'Take Natalie away for the night.'

'What? What are you talking about?'

'I'll book you into a hotel. Spend the night with her. Do whatever it is married couples do. Act like everything's normal.'

'Going away to a hotel for the night isn't normal.' He rolls his eyes and looks at me scathingly. 'For me, at least.'

I turn his face towards mine. 'I said I'm sorry, didn't I? I wish it hadn't happened, but it did. Don't you realise how hard this is for me? I'm telling you to go with her. I'm telling you to sleep with her. If you want Natalie to think everything's normal, you're going to have to make her believe it.'

'We're not even getting on at the moment. She's not going to agree to a night away while we've got the threat of social services hanging over us.'

'Tell her it's what you need, that it'll give you a proper chance to talk everything through. She needs to believe you're a team. Make her believe it.'

But Jake's still reluctant, doubtful that Natalie would even consider it. 'Who'd have Elsie?'

'I will. I'll stay here for the night. She'll be fine.' I kiss him again, for longer this time. 'Do you still want to be with me?'

'You know I do.'

'Then do this. Please. We can work everything out, but you just have to trust me. Do you trust me?'

'I just don't get it. You've wanted me to leave her for ages, so why are you so bothered now if Kara says anything?'

'Because we do it on our terms, not because some jumped-up little city bitch thinks she's got us backed into a corner. You've said yourself it's not the right time. If this comes out while social services are investigating you it'll make everything ten times worse.'

Jake eyes me cautiously, but he knows I'm right. The truth is, we can only get what both of us really wants if Natalie never finds out about us. Any other way will be too complicated, and I've got too much to lose.

'Do you trust me?' I ask him again.

Jake hesitates before answering. 'Of course I do.'

'I'll go and book a hotel now,' I tell him.

We hear the front door. I go to the hallway; the front door is open, and a moment later Kara appears in the doorway, returning for more of her things. She stops when she sees me.

'I love him,' I tell her, but in this moment, neither one of us believes it.

TWENTY-SIX

After getting home from their swimming trip, Natalie and Elsie get back to a quiet house. It was nice to do something normal for an hour, to pretend for a while that they're just like any regular family, but Natalie's worries are never far off, looming over her like an imminent thunderstorm. Jake and Tyler will be out in the fields, and she assumes Kara's upstairs working from her bedroom. They'd stopped at the supermarket after leaving the leisure centre, and now Natalie puts things away while Elsie plays at her wooden kitchen. She's still to talk to Jake about Kara. There never seems to be a right time, and if the two of them are plotting together against her she has to approach this carefully. With social services snooping about, the last thing she needs is more drama.

She goes to the staircase to throw a packet of toilet rolls up the stairs, but before she manages to, Jake appears at the top of the staircase, his overnight bag in his hand. Her stomach lurches.

'Off anywhere nice?' she asks, trying to make her words sound as casual as possible.

'We're going to a hotel for the night. How quickly can you pack your things? We can check in from two o'clock.'

Natalie eyes him with suspicion. They've haven't gone anywhere together for an overnight stay since before Elsie was born, and even then such trips were reserved for birthday treats. Life on the farm is a 24/7 job, and on the rare occasion they've been able to take a break they've always needed to rely on Tyler to look after the place.

'Have you had a bang to the head or something? Have you forgotten everything that's going on?'

Jake bites his lip. 'I thought it would give us a chance to talk.'

'We can do that here.'

Jake carries his bag down the stairs and rests it by the front door. 'Come on,' he says, putting his hands on her shoulders. 'We never get any time together any more.'

'Because you never want it. If I go anywhere near you, you flinch as though I've just burned you.'

She waits for him to deny it, but he can't.

'And what about Elsie?' she says. 'Or had you forgotten about her?'

'Of course I haven't forgotten about her,' he says defensively. 'Tyler's offered to stay here for the night.'

'Which is a very kind offer, but no. You know what Elsie's like – if she wakes and comes into our bedroom she'll be distraught if neither of us is here.'

'She loves Tyler though. She'll be fine.'

'Is there someone else?' Natalie blurts, and as soon as she asks the question she feels so much lighter – so much so that she wishes she'd done it sooner.

She watches his face fall as the words slip from her. 'What? What do you mean?'

'I mean what I say, Jake, it's not a riddle. Are you sleeping with someone else?'

'How can you ask me that?'

'You've not come near me in months. More than months, actually... probably closer to a year. We hardly talk any more. You've been so distant, and now all of a sudden you want us to go and stay in a hotel? It looks like guilt.'

Jake's mouth twists. 'I tell you what then, forget it.' He picks up his bag and throws it up the staircase. 'I can't win, can I? If I don't want to do anything, I'm wrong. When I do want to do something, I'm still wrong. Forget it.'

He walks away, heading for the kitchen. Natalie goes upstairs, kicking his bag out of the way when she gets to the landing. On her way to the bedroom, she passes Kara's door. There's silence from the room: no chatter of a telephone conversation; no tapping of laptop keys. Kara should be working now, but there's no sign that she's here. Natalie knocks on the bedroom door. When there's no response, she opens it. The room's empty. The bed has been stripped and the duvet and pillows have been piled at the headboard. The wardrobe is open, the clothes she saw here just days ago, the boxes she'd looked through, are all gone. The shoes that had been lined up beneath the bed are no longer here. Kara has packed her stuff and gone.

Natalie runs downstairs and checks the side of the house. Kara usually parks in the space near the back of the café; she rarely goes out anywhere in it, so it makes sense for hers to be furthest up the driveway. But, as Natalie has suspected, the car's gone too.

She goes through the kitchen, where she finds Elsie sitting alone. 'Where's Daddy?'

'Out. Get your wellies on, please.'

She follows Elsie to the porch, where she helps her with her wellies. Taking her by the hand, Natalie leads her to the barns. Neither Tyler nor Jake is anywhere to be seen.

'Jake!'

She finds him in one of the barns with Tyler, feeding the cattle.

'Kara's stuff has gone.'

'Has it?'

'Have you seen her? Did she say anything?'

'I haven't seen her,' Jake says, barely raising his head to acknowledge her.

'I never had a good feeling about her,' Tyler says, straightening up to look at her.

Natalie feels stung by the comment. She still wonders how much Tyler knows, and the thought won't leave her alone. He'd made a remark weeks ago, when they were making ice cream together, about the fact it seemed strange Kara had chosen to live here. Was that simply a passing comment, or had Tyler known more than he was prepared to let on? Perhaps he'd been trying to suggest then that Kara was a threat to her.

Jake has been quiet throughout the conversation. His silence sounds like guilt, and now the suggestion of a night away in a hotel seems even more suspicious – an awful attempt to hide the obvious, a truth that Kara's sudden absence is testament to. Natalie wonders whether she's ended the affair, or if it's Jake who's chosen to finish things. No wonder he was so cold towards her that day she came for her first meeting with them. Natalie's mind races with exactly how their relationship might have unfolded. It must have started before Kara came here – how brazen she was to have moved her entire life here, right under the nose of her lover's wife. Perhaps she'd hoped that moving in would help expose their relationship and give Jake the jolt he needed to leave his marriage.

'Can I speak with you please, Jake? Outside.'

Natalie feels herself burn with shame as she walks out of the barn. She's been so naïve. So trusting and ignorant. However the affair came about and however it ended, it's over now. But that's not enough. She can't just carry on as though nothing's happened. It isn't fair on her, and Jake doesn't deserve to have it so easy, not if everything she suspects is true.

'Why's Kara gone?'

'I don't know. I didn't see her before she left.'

'So she just woke up this morning and decided she'd had enough. And then left without speaking to either of us about it? Sounds plausible.'

'I can't speak for her, can I? She's gone. Just leave it there now, please.'

'Were you sleeping with her?'

'What?' he asks, incredulous.

Is he this skilled an actor? she wonders. Can he lie to her face while she's waving the truth in front of him?

'Have you been sleeping with Kara?'

Jake's eyes dart to the barn, conscious that Tyler might overhear the exchange. 'I can't believe you're asking me this.'

'It makes sense though. What did she move here for? Was she hoping it'd give you a push to leave me? Or that I'd find you together?'

'This is mad,' Jake says flippantly.

'Don't do that,' Natalie says, pointing a finger in his face. 'Don't you dare even suggest this is all in my mind. A bit of a strange coincidence, isn't it, that the day she moves all her things out and just leaves without even letting me know she's going is the day you decide you want to spend a night away with me? Or is that just me being mad as well?'

'I didn't say you were mad,' he says defensively. 'I said *it* was mad.'

'You've still not denied it though.'

'I've not been sleeping with Kara, Natalie, for God's sake.'

'Swear it. Swear on Elsie's life that you haven't been sleeping with her.'

'Nat—'

'Do it.'

He hates it when anyone uses another person's name to swear anything by, and she knows he'll hate being asked to use Elsie's. She's never asked him to do it before, yet she's never had any reason before now to do so.

'I've never had any involvement with Kara,' he says, looking her in the eye. 'I swear on Elsie's life, okay? I've never slept with her. Nothing ever happened between us.'

She thought she's known him for long enough to know when he's lying. But what if she doesn't really know him at all?

'Was it Kara who gave Elsie those antibiotics? Did you know about it?'

Jake's face turns dark, his eyes narrowed. 'Are you seriously accusing me of trying to poison my own daughter?'

Natalie feels herself shaking, but she won't be dissuaded. She's justified in thinking it might be a possibility.

'Fuck you, Natalie,' he says, his eyes shining with tears. 'Fuck you!'

He storms back into the barn, kicking a shovel out of his way as he passes. Natalie's heart thunders in her chest. Her heart wants to believe that he's innocent of everything, but her head knows things just don't make sense. Something has been unravelling around her for some time now; she's felt it here, in their home with them, living beside them like another unwanted guest. But Jake wouldn't swear on their daughter's life if he wasn't telling the truth, would he? She wants to believe him, but she doesn't know what to believe any more.

TWENTY-SEVEN

That weekend, when Natalie is at work at the pub, I go back to the farm to speak to Jake. Since Kara's arrival in our lives, the relationship between us seems to have propelled at a pace neither of us could have anticipated, and now she's gone it feels as though there's no turning back. It's now or never for us, and if we have any chance of making this work, I need him to be on side. He has to trust me more than he feels he's able to trust anyone else.

The rain's so heavy I get soaked just getting from the car to the house. Elsie will be in bed by now, and I find Jake in the kitchen, sitting at the dining table with his laptop open in front of him.

'What are you doing back?'

'I needed to see you. We have to talk.'

Jake's least favourite phrase in the world. He avoids any discussion that involves feelings. I used to think his apparent ambivalence was mysterious in an alluring way, that once I got closer to him I'd be able to peel back the layers to find a person only I'd be lucky enough to see and really know. Now, I wonder exactly how much lies beneath. Jake seems less of an enigma these days, more a hollow entity.

'What about?'

I put the file I'm carrying on the table between us before taking out the revised will my mother put together. My mother's been doing the accounts for the farm for years, since Natalie's parents ran the place. She knows the details of the business better than anyone, and last year she helped Jake and Natalie write wills. A couple of months ago, she helped me to redraft Natalie's.

'I need you to look at this.'

I pass the will to Jake, waiting as he reads it. I watch as his face changes, as he tries to make sense of what he's seeing.

'I don't understand. This isn't what was written up with May last year.'

In the original document Mum helped them write, Natalie's will stated that should anything happen to her, ownership of the farm and its entirety would move to Jake. In the event of anything happening to Jake and her – something she was forced to consider in the shadow of what happened to her parents – the farm would be legally Elsie's, with me as trustee until she turned eighteen.

'Any outstanding percentage of the land and relevant finances are to go to Tyler Tandy,' Jake reads. 'What does that mean? "Any outstanding percentage"?'

I take another set of papers from the file: bank statements showing large amounts of cash from the secondary business run from the farm jointly in my name transferred to a personal account in my name. Jake's eyes widen at the numbers: far more money than he'd realised was being made from any of the contracts that have been agreed. They gladly let me take control of a sub-contract supplying milk to a coffee shop chain, not needing the stress of any additional paperwork. Unbeknown to either of them, the deals I managed to strike without them being aware of all the details have always far exceeded their expectations. They've underestimated me, both of them.

'Natalie's letting me buy her out,' I tell him, playing out the rehearsed lines from a script I've been writing in my head for weeks now. 'Bit by bit, until she's got enough money to leave here.'

He doesn't believe it; either that or he doesn't want to bring himself to consider it might be true. He thinks he's the dishonest one in their marriage, but if I'm able to persuade him otherwise, everything could go in my favour. If he believes Natalie's trying to write him out of everything, I can play one against the other, both of them in the dark about how much control they've inadvertently given me.

'The farm's been in her family for generations,' Jake says.

'But she never really wanted it, did she? She was always planning to leave. It was only the accident that kept her here. It's you and me who run this place – Natalie's just been lumbered with owning something she never asked for. She knows this makes sense. She gets to stay in her home while I carry on buying her out,' I continue to lie. 'Once she's got enough money, she can leave. The farm goes to someone she trusts. This way, she doesn't have to live with the guilt of selling out to a stranger. The farm stays in the family, more or less. It works out best for everyone.'

Jake eyes me cautiously. There's irony in my words, but now I'm starting to wonder just how far he believes he can trust me too. He's right to be sceptical: there's no way Natalie would have signed this. That's why I had to trick her into doing it, and she'd made it even easier than I'd been expecting.

I put a hand on his thigh. 'I'm sorry. I know this must come as a massive shock. But she's planning on leaving you, Jake; she has been for months now. Look at how she's been trying to push you away. Accusing you of trying to poison Elsie...'

I don't need to say any more, and I hate the hurt that settles

on his face. Why should it matter to him now whether Natalie
wants to be with him or not? He's been sleeping with me since
we were seventeen, since he first allowed himself to admit what
he'd known from the moment we'd met almost three years
before that. He shouldn't care about her any more. Although
perhaps, like me, it's the thought of losing this place that's
breaking him.

'Whose account is this?' he asks, still disbelieving as he
studies the details.

'Natalie's,' I lie. 'She may have made out like she hasn't a
clue about the finances, but she's been playing us both for fools
for a long time.'

'How could you keep this a secret from me? I've been
working myself into the ground, thinking everything's gone to
shit, and all that time there's been this kind of money floating
about? You've seen how stressed I've been. How could you not
say anything?'

'Because I knew that if I did you wouldn't be able to keep it
from her. And once she knew you knew, it would all be over for
us. She'd keep everything. Look,' I say, taking his hand in mine,
'this is a shock, I know, but once you've had a chance to take
everything in, you'll realise it's the best thing that could have
happened to us. This is our way out.'

Jake looks at me, incredulous. He studies the paperwork
again as though reading his own obituary. 'I don't understand... she wouldn't have signed this.'

'But she did. It's there in black and white.'

Jake continues to read and reread, checking the signature
again.

'I didn't fake it,' I tell him, 'if that's what you're thinking.'

'I wasn't suggesting you did. I'm just... I can't get my head
around it. I thought I knew her.'

'She thinks she knows *you*.' I raise an eyebrow, reminding
him of the charade everyone in this house has been playing out.

'Your marriage is a lie. Your relationship has always been a smokescreen, you know that. But it doesn't have to stay that way.'

'So you get everything,' he says bitterly. 'Where do I fit into all this?'

'You know where you fit in. Here, with me, like you always have.'

'And Elsie?'

'We'll work it out,' I tell him. 'She can't just take your daughter away from you.' I kiss him, long and hard on the mouth, reminding him of who really loves him. 'Natalie's already planning to leave you. All this is evidence of that. If she takes Elsie away without a word to you, she's the one who looks bad. Everything will go in your favour. Social services are going to take a dim view of her doing that, especially after what's just gone on. Just keep your head down. Be a good dad. But you mustn't say anything to Natalie yet. If you let her know you know, we could both lose everything.' I hold his face in my hands, willing him to make eye contact, convincing him everything's going to be okay. 'She's playing into your hands here. Can't you see how much easier this makes things for us?'

Jake starts to cry unashamedly – heavy, wrenching sobs that wrack his body. I put my arms around him and pull him in close, repeating the mantra that everything will be okay; that while we've got each other we can get through anything. He softens in my arms as he starts to believe it, yet no matter how many times I say the words, I can't bring myself to be convinced of them. The truth is, Jake's always been the one who's held me back. And as much as I might have once loved him, I can't let him hold me back any longer.

TWENTY-EIGHT

When Natalie picks Elsie up from nursery on Monday, the manager takes her to the other side of the yard, away from the queue of waiting parents. This has never happened before, and the woman's curt professionalism is an immediate red flag.

'Is everything okay?' Natalie takes her daughter by the hand and squeezes it protectively. 'Elsie hasn't been unwell, has she?'

'We've noticed some bruising to Elsie's arms.' The nursery manager smiles at Elsie reassuringly before coaxing her towards her. 'Here.' She slides Elsie's left sleeve up and turns her arm gently outward so that the pale flesh beneath her armpit's exposed. Natalie hasn't seen the bruises before. They look new, sickly green and small, round. Fingertip bruising.

'Is everything okay at home?'

Natalie feels the colour race to her cheeks in a rush of heat. Has that social worker been here as well, talking to Elsie's teachers?

'Everything's fine,' she snaps. 'I don't like the implication, though.' She crouches to Elsie's side and points at the horse chestnut trees that line the edge of the field surrounding the nursery's grounds. 'Co-comes!' Elsie shouts excitedly – the pronunciation of conkers that until today has always managed to put a smile on Natalie's face.

The manager catches her eye and smiles again, treating Natalie with the same kid-gloves treatment she just gave her daughter. She's looking at her just as Caroline did when she came to the house to snoop around. But Natalie isn't a child: she won't be placated with insincere sentimentality, especially not when she's being accused of harming her own child.

'We know you've been under a lot of pressure recently—'

'Just what are you suggesting? That I've abused my daughter?' Has she spoken with the doctor? Natalie wonders. But that's impossible – it would be a breach of patient confidentiality, surely. But it seems to have happened once already. And what if social services have been in touch with the nursery? Perhaps they've asked the school to keep an eye on Elsie for any signs of abuse or neglect.

'Nobody's saying that. But our responsibility is for the safeguarding of children in our care, and I can't ignore any signs of—'

The manager cuts herself short this time, realising she's gone too far.

'The bruising could have been done by another child,' Natalie says. 'It could have been a member of staff.' She raises an eyebrow, hoping her point's been made loud and clear. This woman won't like the insinuation any more than Natalie did.

'I can assure you,' the woman says haughtily, 'that the children in our care are looked after in an exemplary manner.'

'And I can assure you that Elsie is treated with exemplary care while she's at home with me.'

Natalie calls Elsie back to her and takes her by the hand. 'Come on, sweetheart. We're going home.'

She walks away with such anger pulsing through her that she feels she might not ever go back to the nursery again. There are other childcare facilities available to them, and though they're all further to travel she would rather the inconvenience of that than leave her daughter with people who suspect she's capable of harming her.

'Mrs Prosser,' the teacher calls after her. Natalie turns to see the woman waving an envelope out to her. 'This came for you. We wouldn't usually accept mail addressed to parents, but I made an exception. Please ask whoever it's from not to contact you through us in future.'

The padded envelope is addressed to Natalie Prosser, c/o Elsie Prosser, The Meadows Nursery, St Mary's Street, Llanafan, Carmarthenshire. There's clearly something apart from a letter inside, but Natalie waits until they're back at the car and Elsie's strapped into her car seat before opening it to see what it is. A USB stick. She opens the folded letter that accompanies it, handwritten.

Dear Natalie,

I'm sorry I left without saying goodbye, but when you watch this video I hope you'll understand why I had to. Destroy this letter once you've read it – do not take it home with you. Please make sure you keep the USB stick hidden somewhere safe and don't let anyone know you have it. My intention is not to hurt you – it's to help you. You mustn't let them know you know. For yours and Elsie's sake, you must act as though everything's normal. Call me when you're able to and we'll meet somewhere to talk. You're not on your own.

Kara x

With shaking hands, Natalie reads the letter again, and then a third time. *You mustn't let them know you know.* But who is 'them'? She starts the car. From the back seat, Elsie asks for something to eat, the word 'snack' repeated on a loop until

Natalie eventually finds a forgotten box of raisins squashed in the bottom of her bag.

'We'll get some lunch when we get home, okay?'

She barely absorbs a detail on the drive home. Familiar roads and lanes merge into a blur of green hedge and grey sky, looking less and less recognisable the closer she gets to home. Home. The word triggers a spark in her brain that burns and pulses, setting her thoughts alight. She's scared of what she'll find when she gets back to the farm. She is terrified of what she might see when she looks on the USB stick.

Natalie puts down the window, allowing a blast of cold air to circulate around the car. She glances at the USB stick on the passenger seat. She could throw it into a hedge. All it would take is a moment. She could stop the car and push the note through the bars of the next drain in the road.

She stops the car near a lay-by and reaches for Kara's letter. *Don't let them know you know.*

Them.

'I'm cold, Mama. It's too cold.'

She shoves the letter into her coat pocket and closes the window, and Elsie falls into a contented silence. Natalie tastes bile in the back of her throat as she pushes into first gear. This is wrong, she thinks. She's made an awful mental leap. But the USB stick stares at her from the passenger seat. She'll find out soon enough.

When she gets back to the farm, Jake's not at the house. He's usually outdoors at this time of day, and it gives her a chance to go to the bedroom for her laptop. Back downstairs, Elsie's in the process of removing the scuffed shoes she wears to nursery, a pair that were patent and shiny-new just a couple of months earlier.

'Put them back on,' Natalie says hurriedly, her laptop wedged under one arm as she crouches to help her daughter.

'Why? Where are we going?'

'Do you fancy an ice cream?'

Elsie's little face lights up. Natalie goes to the freezer in the kitchen and takes out a strawberry Cornetto – Elsie's favourite, usually reserved for post-Sunday lunch or as a special reward for extra good behaviour. She unwraps the wafer cone from its paper wrapper and passes it to an expectant Elsie, who manages a quick thank you before tucking in.

'Come on,' she says. 'Let's go and eat it in the café.'

Natalie takes Elsie by the hand and leads her through the back door and across the gravelled driveway. In the café, Elsie sits on one of the smaller chairs while Natalie sets up her laptop on the serving counter. She's already planned her excuses for being there should Jake happen to come by: she'll tell him she's ordering stock in preparation for reopening the shop for the beginning of March. She waits impatiently for the laptop to load. Elsie makes short work of her Cornetto, and once she's done Natalie takes her to the toilet to wash her hands. As hoped, her attention's then quickly absorbed by the toys in the corner.

With a shaking hand, Natalie inserts the USB stick into the laptop. There's only one file on it, named 'November'. She clicks on it, not allowing herself time to talk herself out of looking at what she knows is about to rip the floor from beneath her. When she opens the video, she finds herself looking at her own landing. She observes her house from a strange angle, too close to the floor. The camera's movements are jerky as it's carried to her bedroom door. Natalie wipes a palm hurriedly across each eye, swallowing back imminent tears. Whatever comes next, she's ready for it. She has to be, for Elsie's sake.

She watches as the bedroom door's opened. She sees a tangle of bare legs, observing silently as one pair's frantically extricated from another. Her stomach churns; she tastes sickness in the back of her throat. She sees Jake first, his tousled hair shimmery with sweat. He stands quickly, retrieves his clothing from the floor, and then she sees Tyler as the camera moves back.

A sob escapes her like a gunshot, so loud it breaks Elsie's attention from the toy train she's been manoeuvring in circles for the past few minutes. She remembers Tyler's words, at Halloween, when she'd confided in him that she thought Jake might be having an affair.

Jake would never look at another woman.

'Mama?'

Her best friend: the person she trusts most in this world; perhaps even more than she has trusted Jake.

'It's nothing,' she says quickly, the word breaking against the betrayal that floods her. 'Everything's fine, sweetheart. I'm fine.'

TWENTY-NINE

When I get home that evening, my mother's sitting at her desk in the conservatory, a file open in front of her. There's a glass of something clear beside it, more likely to be vodka and tonic than water, and a half-smoked cigarette balances precariously on the glass ashtray that's probably been in this house for longer than I have.

'Busy day?' she asks, without looking up from her paperwork.

'Same as any other.'

She reaches to the desk, swipes a piece of paper from a pile and waves it in front of me. 'You never told me Natalie had signed this.'

She holds out the rewritten will, the one Natalie inadvertently signed, believing it to be a renewal contract. This is how close we are. This is how much Natalie trusts me; so much that she gives me the power to do pretty much whatever I choose. Now, Jake's given me the same. And soon, I'm going to choose to steal her life from her; the life that's rightfully mine.

'Slipped my mind.'

Neither of Natalie's parents had left a will. Tom was only

forty, Jayne just thirty-eight, and presumably both had thought themselves young enough to not have to worry about such things. As their only child, Natalie automatically inherited everything. It was a responsibility she wasn't prepared for and never really wanted. Some might say I'm doing her a favour in fact.

'Why are you going through my things, anyway?' I ask, though when I'd brought the will back from the farm I hadn't gone to any efforts to hide it.

'How did you get her to do it?' she asks, ignoring my question.

'Does that matter?'

My mother must have known when she'd helped me word the amended copy what my intentions were – why else would she have gone ahead with it if she wasn't every bit as corrupt as I am.

Take what's yours – those had been her words. But why? Why is she as keen as I am to let me get my hands on that farm? If anyone found out what we'd done, she'd at best lose her job. She'd never be able to work as an accountant again, something she's done for her closest clients since her retirement, to keep her occupied. At worst, she could be sent to prison. We both would be. But I still have time on my side, something she doesn't have. I could serve out my sentence; I could rebuild my life. It would be too late for her. Why is she willing to risk everything?

Take what's yours.

'Why was Tom here that night?'

My mother continues to look through the window, her focus fixed on the garden. But I see her hand quiver, the pen she's still holding shaking slightly in her grip.

We've talked about that afternoon, when I came home from school and found Dad hanging on the landing, the noose attached to the attic hatch. The memory is ingrained in my brain. Sometimes still, fourteen years on, I have nightmares so vivid that I wake believing he's there in the room, his work boots hanging above me as I lie in bed. I was thirteen years old. Mum was out somewhere. I shouted out as I went into the house, but there was no answer, so I ran up to my room to get changed. At first, I froze. Then I wet myself. I changed before I went to the neighbour's house to get help; later, someone asked why I'd taken off my school uniform before I'd gone to raise the alarm. I didn't want to admit to anyone that I'd wet myself, so I told them I hadn't been thinking straight, that I didn't know what I was doing.

'That night that Dad was out,' I say, 'and you didn't realise I'd come home.'

It was ten days before Dad died. Mum thought I was over at a friend's house, which I had been until we'd argued. He'd called me something – I don't remember what now. I was called so many names during those first couple of years at the comprehensive that they all began to merge into one long insult. I never stood up for myself, and I'd wondered after my father's death whether he'd been ashamed of what I'd become as I'd got older; whether he'd hoped for more of a lad's lad, the kind of teenage boy who played football and could look after himself in a fight. Instead, I was quiet. I kept myself to myself, a target for the bullies, some of whom I'd thought were my friends. When Jake started at the school, it was the first time I'd truly accepted who I was. He changed me, and I loved him for it.

When I'd gone in through the back door that night, ten days before his death, I'd heard raised voices. There was a man in the living room, but it wasn't Dad. It took a moment to realise it was Tom.

'We've talked about this before.'

We have, but whether or not she's told me the truth is another matter.

'You were arguing over something to do with the accounts,' I say, repeating what she's always told me whenever the subject of that evening has arisen.

She says nothing. This is her go-to response for anything she finds uncomfortable or doesn't want to have to deal with, much like Jake. I've surrounded myself with cowards.

I'd known for ages afterwards that my mother had lied, but like a toddler with his fingers in his ears, I didn't want to hear the truth. I did whatever I could to get away from my own thoughts: skipped school, got into trouble; had a lot of sex, most of it with men a lot older than I was. Eventually, it was enough to drown the nagging echo that taunted me at the back of my head, my mother's voice ringing on repeat.

I was going to tell you.

When? Tom's reply comes now, as though he's here in the room with us. *When were you planning on telling me?*

I repeat the words now, aloud, watching May's face for signs of a reaction. She looks down at her hands, her grip tightening around the pen, her knuckles turning white.

The mind is a powerful thing. It can retain what it chooses, holding on to certain details so tightly that they're never allowed to fall from a person's consciousness, and then just as easily, it can let things go. Memories can be altered or averted. Entire conversations can be pushed into a corner somewhere they can go ignored, because ignorance is preferable to knowledge when that knowledge is something too painful to accept. I'm no different to my mother and Jake. No better. Perhaps I'm the coward, too scared to finally have to face up to what I didn't want to see.

A landslide of ignored opportunities thunders upon me. Dad's silence the morning before he took his own life, how he'd moved through our usual morning routine barely casting me a glance. Later, I'd looked back on that day and thought his distance an indicator that he'd already decided what he was going to do. Perhaps I was right, though now there's something else as well. He couldn't look at me. I'd always thought it was my fault, that I'd disappointed him somehow, but maybe I wasn't the one who was guilty of that.

'Was Tom my father?'

My mother flinches at the question, but her reaction tells me everything I need to know.

'Say it. Say it!'

I swipe the paperwork from the desk, and her body braces itself in the shadow of my violence. She's no idea what I'm capable of. She has no idea what she's made me.

'That's why Dad killed himself,' I say. 'Because he found out.' I feel my jaw tighten as the blood pounds in my ears. 'All those times we talked about that day. All those times I told you I'd known there was something wrong because the day before he did it, he could barely look at either of us. I thought it was guilt, that he already knew he was going to do it, but it wasn't that, was it? He couldn't bear to look at me, like I'd done something. And you knew. All these years I've wondered what I did to make him leave us, and all the time you knew.'

May reaches for her glass but I snatch it from her. 'You don't get to play the victim any more.'

I throw the glass against the wall where it smashes into pieces on the floor. 'Poor May,' I say. 'Widowed so young, at such a young age.'

'Tyler—'

'Shut up! There's nothing you can say to make this better. My whole youth was fucked up by you, because you were too much of a coward to admit what you'd done. How long did it go on for?'

'Not long.'

'Long enough though. Long enough to bring me into your mess. Did Jayne know?'

My mother shakes her head. I'd already guessed as much; she would never have had me working at the farm, practically living there as part of the family, if she'd known that I was her husband's son. Part of the family. The words hit me in the gut. Tom always made a point of reminding me how welcome I was. Like the son they'd never had. The sibling for Natalie they'd always wanted. And Jayne was stupid enough not to see what was going on right under her nose. Like mother, like daughter.

'All those comments you've made in the past about Jake being a married man. You're a hypocrite, you know that? At least what we've got is real.'

'Is it? Are you sure about that? Is it Jake you really want, or is it just that farm?'

Her words burn, but I don't need to justify or explain myself to her. Not any more. I turn to leave but May stands quickly and grabs me by the arm. I shove her from me, and she falls back against the table.

'Don't touch me,' I tell her. 'You're dead to me.'

THIRTY

Natalie calls the nursery the following morning before leaving the house and asks whether they can keep Elsie for the full day today, rather than just for the morning session as usual. She hates to leave her there after the accusation that was made against her, but she has no choice: she's arranged to meet with Kara, and while she doesn't plan their time together to be lengthy, she needs to see her. They need to talk.

She knows too well what grief feels like, and since yesterday she has felt herself mourning her friendship with Tyler as though it were a living thing. She has moved through the motions of it: the denial, the anger, the resentment; the heart-crushing sadness of what now feels a decades-old lie. In so many ways, Tyler's betrayal seems worse than Jake's. She has loved him like a brother. They have shared their whole lives together.

She tries to focus on what needs to be done, and she meets Kara half an hour from the village, in a little town called Abertwyn. There's a quiet stretch of woodland used mostly by dog walkers and joggers, and, as it's usually quiet there, Natalie figures they can talk without interruption or anyone overhearing their conversation. She has been the one to instigate the meeting. After watching that video, everything was flipped on its head. Everything she'd believed about Kara was undone, and now she doesn't know what to think about anyone or anything.

When she gets there, she waits in the car park, watching the entrance for Kara's car. She arrives a couple of minutes later, and when she gets from the car she's dressed for the cold November day, with a knee-length puffer coat and a bobble hat. She apologises as soon as she sees Natalie, as though Jake and Tyler's affair is somehow her fault.

'I'm so sorry, Natalie.'

Natalie doesn't reply. She can't find the words. Since watching that footage, she has avoided both Jake and Tyler while she's tried to work out what she's going to do. She can't just tell them she knows; all their lives would implode. If it was just her, maybe she'd allow that to happen, but she's got Elsie to think about and she has to keep her protected. Despite everything he's done, Jake's still her father, and Elsie is too young and vulnerable to have to deal with the fallout of the mess he's made of everything.

And then there's the thought that Jake might fight her for custody. He has taken everything from her. She will not let him take their daughter.

'When did you find out?'

'The morning I left. You'd gone swimming with Elsie, and —' She stops mid-sentence. She doesn't need to remind Natalie of anything.

'But you must have suspected something was going on before that? Otherwise you wouldn't have—' She can't speak the words, too racked with nausea to make sense of anything. 'How did you film them?'

'Camera in the eye of one of Elsie's teddy bears. I've had to do it before, unfortunately. Not for anything like this. One of the so-called carers at my dad's nursing home.'

'Were they caught out?'

Kara nods. 'And struck off.'

'I'm sorry.'

Kara gives a slight shake of her head, not wanting to talk any more about it. 'I saw the way Tyler looked at Jake. From the first time we met, there's been something about him I've not trusted. I'm sorry, Natalie, I know none of this is what you want to hear.'

She's right about that, at least, but Natalie knows what she wants and what she needs are two very different things. She needs to hear the truth, and she needs to see what else she's been missing. She can't shake the feeling that if Kara was able to see what was going on between Jake and Tyler she should have been able to as well. It shames her that she could have been so naïve and blinded.

'I've known for a while something was going on,' she says. 'I mean, I thought Jake was having an affair. I thought it might have been with you.'

Kara looks crushed by Natalie's words. 'God,' she finally says. 'I'm so sorry.'

'What are you sorry for?'

'Did I ever give you reason to believe there was something going on between us?'

'I thought so,' Natalie admits. 'That night I came back late from the pub and you were drinking together, I think that's where it started. But it was all my own misguided assumptions. I was right to suspect him. I just got the wrong person.'

'I'm so sorry if you ever thought I was inappropriate with Jake.'

Natalie shakes her head. The repeated apologies are becoming annoying. She might have got things wrong about Kara being involved with Jake, but there's still the matter of those sex toys in the wardrobe. She might be naïve in so many ways, but even Natalie knows enough to realise there were an awful lot of items there to be simply for personal use.

'I saw the boxes in your wardrobe,' she says, knowing she has to raise the subject. 'I saw what was in them.'

Kara responds with silence. Perhaps she feels ashamed of what Natalie's found, or maybe she feels affronted by the knowledge her landlady was snooping around among her things. In the same position, Natalie doubts she'd be too happy about it.

'You don't work in IT, do you?' Natalie asks. She sounds more frustrated with herself than she does with Kara, mindful once again that her naivety has allowed her to be blindsided. Is anyone prepared to tell her the truth about anything any more? 'How do you earn a living?'

'Please hear me out before you make a judgement,' Kara says quickly. 'I'm sorry I lied to you. I couldn't tell you the truth – you would never have let me stay.'

Natalie raises an eyebrow, still waiting for an answer. Kara's response has managed to make her suspicions worse.

'I sell content on an adult website. Photographs... videos. I do livestreams, sometimes.'

There's silence as Natalie absorbs the admission. She doesn't know how she's supposed to react or what she's meant to say. What Kara does is her business, yet this was going on in her home, while her daughter was in the house.

'You mean, you sell photos of yourself? You... do things, online?'

Christ, she thinks. Listen to yourself, Natalie. She sounds like an idiot. No wonder Jake and Tyler were able to walk all over her.

'I told you I had to quit university to look after my father when he became too ill,' Kara says. 'That was the truth. I needed a way to make money, something I could do from home that would earn me enough to be able to stay and care for him. I'd read about this site, but I never thought it'd take off like it did. I found myself making more in a week than I could make in a month in any other job, and there was nothing else from home that would make that sort of money.' She pauses, searching Natalie's face for judgement. 'I don't like what I do,' she tells her. 'I did it because I didn't have a choice.'

'But you've been doing it in my home. You were posing for these photographs... you were...' Natalie presses her fingertips between her eyes. She doesn't know how to put it into words, or perhaps she just doesn't want to. There are all kinds of weirdos out there, she thinks; God only knows what Kara might have been requested to do. 'My three-year-old daughter was in the house.'

'My door was always locked,' Kara tells her, though she must know this makes no difference to the indignation Natalie feels at the lie she's been told. Whichever way she skews it, Kara moved in under false assumptions.

'Moving here was meant to be a fresh start for me. I needed space to clear my head, get away from the memories of my dad's illness and from my ex. I'm planning to go back to study law at some point; that's always been the plan. But now, knowing what I do about Jake and Tyler, I can't leave here, Natalie. I want to help you.'

'I don't need anything from you, Kara. We were happy before you came here.'

'No, you weren't. You were living a lie.'

The words are a punch to Natalie's gut, even though she knows they're true. How long might she have remained ignorant about what's been going on? And a worse thought yet... just how much more is Tyler responsible for?

'I don't need your help,' she says between gritted teeth, fighting back tears she doesn't want Kara to see. 'I'm surrounded by liars I thought were my friends. I don't know who any of you are. I'm sorry, I can't do this.'

She walks away, and Kara doesn't try to follow her. By the time she gets back to the car, she's half-blinded with tears.

Everything's a mess, and she has no idea any more who she can trust. The only reliable person in her life is Elsie, but the thought makes her feel even more isolated. How is she going to start their lives again, free from everything Jake's brought down upon them? Does she need to keep her daughter safe from both him and Tyler?

On the drive home, Natalie's mind plunges into free fall. Does May know about the affair between Jake and Tyler? He's closer to her than anyone, and though they've not always got on, she's still his mother. She's known Natalie's family for years, since before she and Tyler were born. May knows their business and their finances probably better than Natalie does. They've trusted her with their life.

By the time she gets home, she's emotionally exhausted. She doesn't know how she's going to put on a pretence in front of Jake and Tyler, but she knows she can't reveal anything, not yet. All the things she'd wondered whether Kara might have been guilty of, she now suspects of Tyler. Just how dangerous might he be?

The thought that Tyler might be responsible for giving Elsie the antibiotics that have made her unwell makes her sick to her stomach. He is family. The closest person to an uncle Elsie has. Yet it all seems so clear now: so much so that she chides herself for being so naïve. She's trusted Jake with the farm and their lives, and she's trusted Tyler with the same. Now, she realises what a terrible mistake that has been. He's welcome to her husband, but he's never going to get his hands on Natalie's daughter or their home.

She goes out onto the fields to find them, knowing she can only avoid them for so long. The last thing she wants either of them to believe is that she's frightened of them. Whatever they're planning between them, she must appear to be one step ahead, even if she's not.

'Where's Elsie?' Jake asks.

'I asked the nursery to keep her for a full day. I've got some admin to finish up.'

Tyler approaches. 'Mum's having one of her episodes,' he says.

'She okay?' Natalie asks.

Tyler rolls his eyes. 'You know what she's like. Her own worst enemy.'

May's 'episodes' have ranged from weekend-long drinking sessions to a twelve-week stint in rehab, during which time a teenage Tyler had lived with Natalie and her family at the farm. The thought drives a flame of rage burning through her. They gave him everything, and this is how he's repaid them.

Natalie looks at Jake. His focus remains on the cattle feed, despite the task seeming to be complete. She sees it now where she hasn't before. All those times she's thought him deep in concentration, a hard worker, determined and focused on his job, she realises she was duped. He keeps his focus on anything so he doesn't have to look at Tyler. Jake isn't conscientious. He's a coward.

'Jake's said I can stay for a few nights. There's the spare room now Kara's gone. You don't mind, do you? You know how it is, I can't do anything right while she's like this.'

Natalie knows exactly how it is. Tyler and May have had arguments in the past that have bordered on violence, their relationship as volatile as it is fragile. She'd always assumed May's drinking was responsible for their rows, but what if that hasn't really been the case? She feels her pulse quicken. She doesn't want him here. She can't trust him. She's no idea what he might be capable of, or just how much he's already done. But if she shows him this, she may trigger something they'll all come to regret.

Don't let them know you know.

'Of course, that's fine. Have you got everything you need?'

Tyler nods. 'I'm fine.' He comes closer to her and puts his

hands on her shoulders. 'Thank you. You're too good to me. I don't deserve it.'

He closes her in a hug, and Natalie feels her body tighten. She feels sure he must sense it too.

'Thanks, Nat,' he says, pulling away from her, his eyes holding hers for longer than is comfortable. 'Just what would I do without you?'

THIRTY-ONE

For three nights I've seen Kara at a B & B in Abertwyn, a small village about twenty minutes away from Llanafon. After leaving the farm each day, I've gone there to watch for her, seeing her return to the house with shopping or talking at the front door with the owner of the building, an elderly woman who looks too old and frail to be running the place on her own. I've no idea why Kara's still here in Carmarthen, but if my first warning wasn't enough for her, I'm going to need to make myself a little clearer this time.

I arrive just after 2 p.m. Kara's car's parked on one of the side streets, so I know she's here. I grab the flowers I bought from the florist on the high street from the passenger seat and lock the car, making my way to the steps of the B & B entrance. I ring the doorbell. The owner answers. She's in the middle of cleaning by the looks of things, wearing an apron with a cloth tucked into the pocket.

'For me?' she says, looking at the bouquet with a smile. 'It's been a long time since a good-looking young man bought me flowers.' She laughs, the sound followed by a splutter of smoker's cough.

'Actually, I'm looking for my girlfriend,' I tell her. 'Kara. She said she'd be in this afternoon.' I choose the fattest rose and slide its stem from the bouquet. 'She won't miss one,' I say with a wink, and I pass her the flower.

'Ooh, you're a charmer.' She takes the rose and tucks it lengthways beside the cleaning cloth. 'Go on with you,' she says, ushering me into the hallway with a smile. 'Room three on the second floor. Tell her I said she's a lucky lady.'

'It's me who's the lucky one.'

I go up to the second floor, leave the flowers outside the next room and tap at the door. Kara won't be expecting anyone; she'll probably think I'm the scatty cow who's just let me up here. There's no spy glass in the door, but I stand aside anyway, waiting for her to open it.

She doesn't have time to react when she sees me. I grab her with one arm wrapped around her chest and put a hand over her mouth as she tries to fight me off. We stumble into the room and I kick the door shut behind me, Kara desperately clawing at me, fighting to break loose.

'I've got a knife in my pocket,' I tell her. 'Stop trying to fight me.'

Kara continues to writhe in my grip, but the more she fights, the harder I hold her. Realising I'm too strong for her, she begins to soften; I feel her fall limp beneath my hold as she relents. But I'm not stupid. She's a devious bitch, and whatever she's planning I'll be ready for her.

'Why are you still here?' I ask her, though she's unable to answer, my hand still over her mouth. 'I'm going to let you go, okay? But try anything stupid and I won't think twice about hurting you.'

When I let her go, Kara lunges for the lamp on the side table. She swings it at me, but I'm faster than her and, as I move to the side she falls forward, dropping the lamp as she loses her footing against the end of the bed. I slam into her and pull the knife from my pocket as I drop my body on top of hers. She is beneath me now, pinned to the bed.

'You need to leave here today. Pack up your shit and get back to wherever you came from.'

She tries to smile in an attempt at defiance, but her fear's so strong I can practically taste it in the air. She's no idea what I'm capable of, and she's only just starting to let herself imagine the possibilities.

'I'm not scared of you.'

'Then you're more of an idiot than I realised. How about I call the police and tell them you took Elsie from her bed and left her in the lane.'

Kara's face changes as my words take shape to form a picture in her brain. I see her eyes flash as the visions alter and the realisation of what happened that night drops like a stone. The atmosphere between her and Natalie had been strained after that night, the two of them seeming to avoid one another. I could never mention anything without giving myself away, so I stayed quiet, but I always wondered what Kara had been doing out so late that night, and where she'd been. Natalie got lucky that Kara was there. If she hadn't been, anything might have happened.

'People all know each other around here,' I remind her. 'They don't take too kindly to strangers.'

'You were the reason Elsie was out there that night?'

I'd sat in one of the barns and watched it all unfold. Natalie woke because I wanted her to; I made a noise outside the living room window, though I don't think she remembers this. She'd had a cocktail of sleeping tablets and antidepressants strong enough by then for her memory to have been affected, so I've never been too sure exactly what she remembers of that night.

'I know the local police quite well,' I tell Kara. 'They looked out for me when my dad died. Who do you think they're going to believe? And once everyone gets to hear about your job... the real one, not the bullshit IT one you've made up for Natalie's sake, I don't think you'll have much credibility left, do you?'

'You bastard,' she says quietly.

'Which story do you think will work better? That you tried to abduct her? Or that you'd become so obsessed with Jake you wanted to punish Natalie? A or B – you pick.'

She looks nervously at the knife in my hand. She knows I'll use it if I'm pushed hard enough.

I lean towards her, the knife edge tipped towards her chest. 'Wear that black lacy outfit for me again, FitGirl94,' I say tauntingly. 'Like last time.'

She tries to fight back tears as she realises just how much of her I've seen. I know her username for the site she works from, and now I watch her eyes as she understands what happened just a few days before she left the farm. I was the one at the other side of her laptop screen. I gave her instructions, and she did everything I told her to; now, she's going to do the same again.

'Turn around.'

'Tyler, please,' she says, begging now. 'Don't hurt me. I'll go. I won't say anything to anyone, I promise.'

I point the knife at her again and repeat the instruction. 'Do it, Kara. I'll make it quick, I promise.'

She sobs as she gets up and turns on the bed. 'Tyler, don't do this. You'll lose everything. You'll lose Jake.'

I yank her ponytail and pull her head back. Her pale throat's exposed, and I can feel her whole body shaking through her hair. I bring the knife back, but then the bedroom door opens. The B & B owner screams. Kara dives across the bed and I drop the knife; I knock the woman over as I run for the door, sending her slamming to the landing floor. There's screaming behind me, but it fades as I make it downstairs and out onto the street. My chest burns with panic. I should have killed the bitch while I had the chance, but I couldn't do it with a witness there. I'll have to deal with the old lady later, one way or another. I console myself with the thought that all my fury is wasted on Kara. There's someone else far more deserving.

THIRTY-TWO

Natalie watches Tyler as he flees the B & B. For the past three days since he's been staying at the farm she's kept herself out of the way as much as possible, feigning migraines and taking Elsie out so that neither of them has to be around him and Jake. She knew when Tyler left the farm that afternoon that he was plotting something, her gut telling her he was looking for Kara. She watched him go in with a bouquet of flowers, the foolish B & B owner apparently charmed by his bullshit. Just as she's been, she thinks, all these years.

She waits to see his car leave the end of the street and then she runs across the street and into the B & B.

'Kara! Kara!'

She hears voices upstairs, then Kara's voice calling to her. On the landing, she finds her crouched beside the B & B owner who's stretched out on the floor. 'Is she okay?'

'I'm fine,' the woman tells her. 'I just can't get up, that's all.'

Natalie and Kara take an arm each, gently helping the woman onto her feet.

'Who was that madman?' she asks. 'I'm calling the police.'

'No,' Kara blurts. 'That won't be necessary.' She shoots

Natalie a glance that silences her. She understands. If the police are involved now, everything will get worse. There's no proof of anything yet, other than that Jake and Tyler are having an affair. If they want evidence of Tyler's guilt, they're going to have to stay quiet for a while longer.

'I'm so sorry,' Kara says, helping the B & B owner into her bedroom and sitting her on the chair at the dressing table. 'We were just, you know. Things got out of hand.'

The woman looks at her with a blank expression, with apparently no idea what she's referring to.

'I promise you it wasn't what it looked like.'

'It looked to me like the lunatic was going to kill you!'

Kara laughs lightly, as though the whole thing is some kind of joke. She turns to Natalie for support, silently willing her to play along with it. 'He's my boyfriend. God,' she adds, with a performance Natalie finds unnerving. 'This is embarrassing.' She looks back to the B & B owner and lowers her voice conspiratorially. 'We were role-playing.'

The woman purses her lips as though she's sucking on a lemon. 'I've heard it all now. That's how people get their kicks nowadays, is it? So what's he run off for then, if he wasn't trying to slit your bloody throat?'

Natalie looks at Kara with horror as she realises now what the old lady had interrupted. But Kara gives a slight shake of the head, willing her to continue with the false version of events she's constructing.

'You shocked him, that's all. You shocked us both.'

'I want you out of here,' the woman says, standing. 'Now. I'm not having that sort of nonsense in my house. It's disgusting.'

Kara's eyes continue to plead with Natalie to stay silent. The woman goes to the bedroom door. 'You've got ten minutes to pack your stuff up, or I'm calling the police.'

'What did he do to you?' Natalie asks as soon as the

bedroom door's shut. She doesn't really need to ask. There are signs of bruising already on Kara's neck. 'Shit, Kara. Are you okay?'

'He's dangerous, Natalie. You need to get out of there. You and Elsie.'

The marks on Kara's neck hold Natalie transfixed. She thinks of the bruises the nursery manager showed her on Elsie's arm, small and round. Fingertip bruising. Not Tyler, she tries to tell herself. But if he's capable of administering her meds meant for the cattle, he's capable of doing anything.

'I'm so sorry, Kara.'

'None of this is your fault. Don't let him or Jake make you start believing that it is.'

Kara sits on the edge of the bed, her eyes darting to her reflection in the mirror that sits on the dressing table. 'That night in the lane, the night I found Elsie outside. It was Tyler. He's just admitted to it. He took her from her bed. He's just threatened to tell the police I did it, that I'm obsessed with Jake or some crap.'

Natalie's head swells with the other woman's words. She'd seen Tyler out that night; she had locked the door. But he had a key. Tyler has had a key to the house since he was a teenager. After his father took his own life, Tyler had spent most of his time outside of school at the farm, Natalie's parents telling him that the spare bedroom was there for him whenever he wanted it. Not long after that, he'd needed it when May had gone into rehab.

Kara goes to the chest of drawers and begins shoving her belongings into her suitcase.

'But why?' Natalie asks, finally managing to speak. 'Anything might have happened to her. Why would he do that?'

'To get to you,' Kara says. 'I've known men like Tyler before. That fall you had, the day you fainted. You were with him, weren't you?'

Natalie shakes her head. This can't be happening. She'd known she hadn't made a mistake with her medication, but still she'd doubted herself. The headaches, the tiredness, the forgetfulness... suddenly so much seems to make sense. He's been at the farm all the time; he's practically lived there. He's had so much opportunity to spike her drinks and her food. He's had so much opportunity to do the same to Elsie.

Kara goes into the bathroom. The truth seems obvious now, and yet Natalie still doesn't want to believe it. There's a part of her that's as angry with herself for being so naïve as she is with Tyler for being so manipulative and cruel. This can't always have been him; surely no one is born evil. So what happened to him to make him change?

'I don't think he's just after Jake,' Kara says, coming back into the bedroom and putting a cosmetics bag into her suitcase. 'He wants the farm.'

'What? Why would you think that?'

'I've been to his mother's house. May's your accountant, isn't she?'

'How do you know that?'

'I made an appointment with her,' Kara says, ignoring the question. 'I gave her a fake name and everything, in case she mentioned me to Tyler. I didn't have much time, only a few minutes while she went off to make a cup of tea, but it was enough.'

Kara unlocks her phone and goes to her gallery. She scans it briefly before showing Natalie a series of photos, each of documents relating to the farm. It's too much for her to take in properly, but enough for her to see how naïve and trusting she's been.

'Why are you doing all this? Why are you even still here?'

'I had a sister,' Kara says, putting her phone on the bed and getting her suitcase from the bottom of the wardrobe. 'Her name was Hayley.' She gets up and goes to the drawer, where she pulls out a purse. She flips it open and holds it out to Natalie. There's a photograph inside, two girls around the ages of ten sitting side by side on matching bikes, their long hair flat beneath their cycle helmets.

'She got involved with someone older than her when she was a teenager,' Kara continues. 'Dougie Cartwright. So good-looking and charming, at first. Everyone knew he was abusive towards her, but she refused to hear a bad word against him. My father begged her to leave him, but the more he nagged at her, the further from us she drifted. It had been just the three of us for years. My mother died of cancer when I was five. My father sacrificed everything for Hayley and me, his career and the home we'd been in until then. We moved somewhere cheaper so he could stop working, to look after us. We never had much growing up. Those bikes were given to us by one of the neighbours whose twins had outgrown them. But we always had Dad. That's why, when he got unwell, I couldn't let him down. He'd given up everything for us. I couldn't not do the same.' She gestures to the suitcase. 'Will you help me pack?'

'What happened to Hayley?' Natalie asks, as she empties clothes from the drawers. Her mind has fixed itself on Kara's use of the past tense.

'She got pregnant. She didn't tell anyone – we found out afterwards. She fell down the stairs when she was twelve weeks. Dougie found her in the hallway, apparently. That was what he told the police. But he pushed her down those stairs, I know it. That night out in the lane, when I told you I'd been to see a friend, that was the truth. Someone Hayley and I knew from school contacted me to tell me he'd finally been sent down. He'd tried to strangle another girlfriend, but he was interrupted by a neighbour. I saw it in Tyler as soon as I met him. That same darkness. I knew you couldn't trust him.' She puts a hand to her neck, her fingertips touching the bruising made by him. 'I couldn't help Hayley. But I can help you. Please let me help you.'

Natalie's eyes glaze over. Just last week, she'd thought this woman a threat to her family and her marriage. Now, she's the only person in the world Natalie might be able to trust. Yet she knows she can't. Kara isn't here by chance. Her arrival in their lives was the catalyst for everything that followed. It no longer feels an act of fate that she's here in all their lives. And no matter how perfect she tries to make herself appear, Natalie knows she's still lying about something.

'Why are you really here, Kara? Why did you come to live with us?'

Kara reaches to Natalie and takes her hand in hers. 'I'm not going to leave here while you need me. I promise.'

'Why, Kara?' Natalie presses, frustrated by her avoidance of an answer. 'Who are you, really?'

They hear a noise outside the door, then a woman's voice telling them she's about to call the police.

'Go,' Natalie says, passing Kara her suitcase. 'But don't come back to the farm. I don't know who you are. I don't need your help.'

Kara hesitates before leaving.

Natalie follows down the stairs and watches her get into her car before going to her own, wondering whether she's done the right thing. Kara may be her only ally, but there's still something about her that scares her, something she doesn't understand and isn't sure she wants to get to the bottom of. There was a reason Kara told her about her sister, though Natalie can't imagine where she and her family fit into any of this. With a pounding head and the fear that she must now deal with Tyler alone, Natalie's focus returns to Elsie. She needs to get her from the nursery, but while Elsie's still there, at least she knows she's safe. There's time for her to confront May.

THIRTY-THREE

My dad is buried in the graveyard behind the church in the village, just down the road from Elsie's nursery. Every now and then, when I'm feeling up to it, I go to visit him, just to sit and chat, get things off my chest. He knows all about Jake and me. For years now, he's been the only person I've been able to talk to about him without fear of judgement, because even though Mum knows, she's made it clear she doesn't approve. Her hypocrisy makes me sick to my stomach. All this time she's chastised me, and all this time she's been guilty of far worse.

'Why didn't you say something?' I ask him, knowing there's only the two of us here for this one-sided conversation. 'You could have just left her. I'd have understood once I was old enough to get it.'

Usually, I appreciate the silence with which my words are met. I don't want a response or an opinion; I just need to talk, to rid myself of the weight. Today though, I long for the sound of a reply. There might be something he could say to stop me. Or perhaps it's already too late for that.

I kneel on the grass. The cold cuts through my trousers and quickly starts to seep into my skin.

'I've realised something. The things I've done... everything I am... it all comes back to the day you left us. I died that day as well. I think you've always known that. I've done some bad things, Dad. Terrible things. But if life had been different, those things wouldn't have happened. So it's not my fault, really, is it? It's Mum's. It's Tom's.'

In my lap, my hands ball into fists. Like that afternoon I wet myself on the landing, I find I'm crying, incapable of doing anything to stop it. Only this time, I don't care.

'The farm's going to be mine. Do you think Mum will be proud? She wanted me to make something of myself. She's kept reminding me all these years that I should take what was rightfully mine. Well, here I am. Future business owner. Mr Independent. No one will ever be able to take anything from me again.'

It starts to rain. Light drops begin to hit my face and my hair. With every splash that hits my father's headstone, I realise more and more how neglected it's been and how dirty it's become. With guilty fingers, I wipe the moss and the soil from the stone, freeing the engraved words from the filthy mask they've been hidden behind. *Edward Tandy 1967–2009. Loving husband to May. Doting father to Tyler.*

My hands find the ground as I steady myself. I kneel at the graveside as though in prayer, wishing that things could be different and that everything could be undone. But I know regret is futile, and wishes are never granted. No one ever got anything by wishing hard enough for it.

I think of my mother in her conservatory, sitting in her dressing gown, her whisky glass for company. The image fills me with a fury that feels bigger than I am, too strong for me to contain. I recall the day of Dad's funeral; I see a thirteen-year-old me clutching his mother's hand at the graveside as though letting go would mean falling six feet under the ground with him. I knew what she'd done. Deep down, ever since hearing them together in the living room that day, I'd always known about her and Tom, but I'd managed to block it out, never wanting to believe it. Because, without them, who was I able to trust? Who did I have?

'She let me think it was my fault.'

I'd blamed myself for years afterwards, forever wondering what I'd done that was so bad he couldn't bring himself to stay. But it wasn't that Dad couldn't live with me. It was that he could no longer live with *her*. Because this is what women do to men. They drain the life from them. They suffocate them. And, for the past decade, I've watched it happen to Jake. Natalie snared him with a life he'd never wanted, and he's been trapped there ever since. The only escape he's ever had has been me. I couldn't save my father. But it's not too late for me to save Jake. We can still be happy. I'm the only one who's ever been able to give him what he really wants.

But Jake's already leaving me. He's been distant for weeks now, long before I told him about meeting up with that other man. I should have given him an ultimatum sooner. I should have taken matters into my own hands years ago. I've made him a promise now – I've told a lie I'm not yet sure how I'm going to implement. And yet, there's only one way to go about it. Natalie has to disappear.

I get up and brush the dirt from my knees. The rain is heavier now. 'Bye, Dad. I'll see you again when it's all over.'

Minutes later, I'm at the house. The door is locked. I bang on the glass, waiting for an answer, but she doesn't come. I find my key and let myself in. I go to finish what should have been ended years ago.

THIRTY-FOUR

After leaving the B & B, Natalie heads for the nursery to collect Elsie. She hasn't wanted to send her back there since the manager accused her of some kind of abuse, but she hasn't had a choice. Elsie can't be dragged through all this with her. She needs to be protected. Natalie has to find out the truth, and then she needs Jake to go. She isn't going anywhere: the farm belongs to her. It's Elsie's home. It's Jake and Tyler who need to leave.

Despite what she saw on that footage Kara sent her, there's a part of Natalie that still can't bring herself to believe this is him. She and Tyler have known each other since they were just little kids; they went to the same primary school together and their parents had been friends. Sometimes, at weekends, Tyler's mum and dad would come over to the farm to have dinner with Natalie's parents, and she and Tyler would roam the farm and its surrounding fields and woodland, foraging for berries and daring each other to do things they knew their parents would disapprove of. As a teenager, Tyler got a weekend job on the farm, helping Natalie's dad with the milking and the cleaning out. And then his father died. News of his death had spiralled through the village and beyond. Nothing like it had ever happened around here. There was gossip and small talk, cruel rumours regarding the circumstances surrounding his suicide. It was Tyler who had found him. He'd withdrawn into himself, skipping school and shutting himself off from his friends. The only people who continued as a constant in his life were Natalie's family, her father in particular stepping in to try to guide a young Tyler away from a slippery slope of self-destruction that might have taken his adult life on a very different course.

Tyler has been family for as long as Natalie can remember. She'd cared for him after the accident, staying by his hospital bed for those first few days, refusing to leave his side. With her parents gone, Tyler had been the only family she'd had left. She has given him everything, and this is how he's repaid her.

In the car, she calls May's home number. She doesn't think Tyler will be there; he'll have probably gone back to the farm, and when she gets back there she knows she's going to have to put on the performance of a lifetime. She must, for Elsie's sake. If Tyler realises she knows what he's been doing, all their lives will be in danger. She doesn't want Elsie to witness any of the devastation that's going to undoubtedly ensue. May's house phone rings and rings, eventually going through to the answerphone. *Hello*, May says. *I can't get to the phone right now, so leave a message. If you're after Tyler, try his mobile.*

Does May know about Jake? she wonders. Tyler's lived with her all these years, the farm the only other home he's ever known. Their relationship has always been punctuated by spells in which her drinking drove a gap between them, but they were somehow always able to close it. Were they close enough that he might have confided in her about his affair with Jake?

Kara's words ring in her head. *He's after the farm.*

The thought makes Natalie's head swell with a tangle of anger and betrayal. She thinks of the last time she saw May, when she and Elsie had shared ice cream and coffee with her.

Natalie had been so grateful for her company. May has been so nice to Natalie in recent years, especially since Elsie was born. She doesn't want to think that her kindness was a cover-up for guilt, but perhaps that's what it's been.

Natalie cuts the call, realising the answerphone has already connected and she's been leaving a silent message. She should speak to May in person. She wants to look her in the eye and see her deny that she knew anything was going on between them.

When she gets to the house, the place is silent, with no lights on. She rings the bell, but there's no answer. The thought of Tyler at the farm sends a chill through her. She goes to May's front window and presses her nose to the glass, but the curtains are partially drawn and she can barely make out any of the room. There's no movement from inside. She bangs on the door; calls May's name through the letter box. And then her phone starts ringing in her pocket.

The caller ID is unknown.

'Mrs Prosser? This is Caroline Davies, from social services.'

Natalie feels her heart drop. She'd known this would happen. She'd warned Jake that they hadn't heard the last from this woman.

'Is everything okay?'

'We've received an email regarding Elsie's welfare.'

'What email? From who?'

'There's been a claim made that Elsie was seen out in the lanes near the farm at around two thirty a.m. a couple of weeks ago. Do you know why someone might say this?'

Tyler. All of it comes back to Tyler. He was still there at the farm that night. He had never left. And now this. He wants her to lose everything.

'Mrs Prosser?'

'I'm sorry. I can... look... I know what's going on here, and I think I know who sent you that email. I know who gave Elsie those pills.'

'Was Elsie out in the lanes?' Caroline asks.

'Yes, but it's not what it sounds like. Someone's setting me up. That fall you knew about, when I ended up in hospital, I think he was drugging me like he drugged Elsie, and then there was the crow, and the graffiti, and the ice cream, and—'

'Natalie, you need to slow down a bit.'

'He moved the pot as well, with the rings, and it must have been him who made the call from the hospital, or pretending to be the hospital, and not him but someone he put up to it somehow, and then he must have deleted the call from my phone, it will have been easy enough for him to find out my passcode, he was there all the time, I just never saw any of it because I trusted him, I trusted him with Elsie and I thought it was all Kara's doing, but I realise now how naïve I've been, he just wanted me to believe I was losing a grip on everything but everything seems so clear now.'

She stops talking. She sounds as though she's lost her mind.

There's a silence on the other end of the phone. Finally, Caroline speaks. 'Can we meet to discuss all this in person, Mrs Prosser? It all sounds rather confusing. Do you believe you or Elsie to be in any immediate danger?'

'No,' she says quickly, remembering Kara's warning. The last thing they need is social services turning up again and rousing Tyler's suspicions. She needs him to believe everything's normal, then she needs to get Elsie away from there. 'And yes, please, let's meet in person.'

'I could come to the farm tomorrow morning, at about eleven. Is that suitable for you?'

'Perfect. Thank you.'

She realises now she has no idea just how much Tyler might be responsible for, and just how much influence he must have over Jake. She wonders whether Jake knows about the email Tyler sent to social services. But Jake must trust him implicitly, in the same way she's trusted her husband. He's been having sex with him, she tells herself. They're lovers. Tyler has Jake exactly where he wants him, completely vulnerable to being manipulated and ripped off.

Or maybe that's you, a voice in her head tells her. More likely they're both in on it, working together to ruin her. After all, wasn't that what she'd thought of Jake and Kara? The idea explodes a million memories, shattering everything she'd thought she knew about her past. Details of their rushed wedding fracture in her head like smashed glass. Was any of it ever real? Her husband has been having sex with a man. The man she'd believed was their closest friend. Has she ever really known either of them at all?

Of course she hasn't. Tyler's a man so violent he was about to cut Kara's throat. She needs to get Elsie from the nursery and take her somewhere safe.

She approaches the village welcome sign. The afternoon sky has turned a heavy grey, the threat of the forecasted storm looming ominously above her. By the time she gets to the nursery, it's started raining. There's a queue of parents already at the nursery, hoods up and umbrellas brandished against the downpour. Natalie waits anxiously as each child in turn comes out through the door, the classroom assistant smiling as their carer steps out to meet them. When it finally comes to her, the assistant's face speaks to Natalie before the woman has a chance to open her mouth. Natalie feels her heart drop into her empty stomach.

'Elsie's already gone,' she tells her. 'Tyler collected her.'

THIRTY-FIVE

When Jake comes into the kitchen, I'm already midway through preparing the vegetables. The onions are sharp, and my eyes feel glassy with the sting of them. He looks at me questioningly before going to Elsie, who's sitting at the kitchen table playing on an iPad. He has allowed me to stay here under duress, knowing he doesn't really have much choice. He no longer trusts Natalie and he's terrified of losing Elsie.

'Where's Natalie?' he asks.

'No idea. I can't imagine she'll be long.'

'You picked Elsie up from nursery?'

I see him eye his daughter warily, as though checking for evidence of any harm. He's finally realising he has no idea what I'm capable of.

'Not a problem, is it? She was happy to see me, weren't you, Elsie?'

She doesn't look at me. She hasn't been the same around me since that night she wet herself. I've wondered whether she's ever mentioned anything to Natalie, though I'm sure I'd have heard about it by now if she had.

'I thought we could all have dinner together,' I say with a smile. I go over to him, the knife still in my hand. 'There's wine in the fridge. I've bought a cheesecake – your favourite.'

'What at you playing at, Tyler?'

I raise my hands in mock innocence. 'What? Can't a friend make dinner for his favourite couple?'

His jaw tightens, but he can't do or say anything because Elsie's here in the room with us and she's looking right at him. For all her ignorance, she isn't stupid. She senses something isn't normal; some shift that sits in the air like static. Jake reaches for my arm and leads me back to the worktop, pulling me so both our backs are to Elsie.

'I want you to go,' he says through gritted teeth.

'No.'

He puts a hand on my arm, his fingers digging into my skin, a warning that falls short of any real threat. 'Go,' he says, his voice low. 'Please.'

I turn the knife towards him, its blade edge catching the overhead light. 'We're going to eat dinner,' I tell him. 'All of us. Together.'

He looks me in the eye, but I can see from his reaction he's not sure who he's looking at. He invented a version of me that suited him: the quiet type; the loyal one; the best friend who'd never challenge him, would obediently do whatever he was told. But that isn't me; it never has been. It might have been what he and Natalie wanted to see, but neither of them has ever known me, not really.

I played a long game for both our sakes, but I'm tired now, and it ends tonight.

'I thought we were supposed to be acting normally?' he says, voice lowered.

'That's what I'm doing.' I put down the knife and put my hands on his shoulders before running my fingers across his unshaven face. 'Just think, this is what it can be like every night when it's just the two of us.'

I feel his body stiffen beneath my touch. He looks through me as though he's trying to work out what's going on in my head; as though if he looks hard enough he might be able to find some answers.

Jake turns and looks at his daughter. 'Elsie. Shall we go and get a book?'

But as Elsie gets down from her chair we hear the front door. A moment later, Natalie clatters into the kitchen, coat and boots still on. Her hair's plastered to her head, her jeans soaked through to her skin. Her face is pink with panic.

'Elsie!'

Relief melts her features when she sees her daughter safe and sound. 'You didn't tell me you were going to collect her,' she says to me, and when she makes eye contact I see it there in her eyes. She knows.

'I was passing right by there anyway,' I tell her. 'I did try to ring you. I thought I left a message. Maybe your signal was bad.'

Silence descends upon us. I didn't try calling her, and she knows I'm lying. Jake looks from Natalie to me and back again, and I wonder whether he's thinking the same as I am. He's looking for an escape route, trying to work out how to get them all out of here before anything happens. All three of us know what's coming. Everything's about to unravel.

'I was just about to take Elsie to read a book,' Jake says.

'Don't be too long then,' I say cheerily. 'Dinner will be five minutes.' Jake and Elsie head upstairs. A surge of resentment rushes through me. He's a coward. He must know everything is drawing to some kind of resolution, and his go-to response is to run away, the same as it's always been. But he can't run from this, not this time.

Natalie takes off her dripping coat and hangs it in the porch. 'The storm's picking up,' I say, looking at the darkening evening that lies beyond the kitchen window. The wind rips through the trees at the far side of the driveway as rain batters against the glass. 'Just as well I don't have to drive home.'

Natalie goes to the cupboard and takes out a glass which she fills with water. She drains it all before putting the glass in the sink. 'Is there anything I can do? What are you making?'

She's putting on an excellent performance.

'Chicken stir-fry. I know Elsie may not eat it, so I've done her sausage and mash.'

'Thank you. What's all this for then? I haven't missed a special occasion, have I?'

'Does it have to be for anything? Call it a thank you. For everything you've done for me.'

I move towards her and feel her visibly flinch when I hold her by the shoulders. Has she spoken to that bitch Kara? Just how much has she told her? Everything, I suspect.

When I put my arms around her and hold her, I feel her body brace as though expecting an assault. I think of the way she reacted to me on Halloween – the internal struggle between what she knew was right and what, even just for a moment, she'd been tempted by. The thought of me and her together. What a fucking idiot she must feel now.

'Why don't you go and get changed? You're soaked through. Give Jake and Elsie a shout while you're up there, tell them it's ready.'

I watch her leave and listen to her go upstairs. I wonder whether she'll tell Jake now that she knows, though I doubt it; he's not as skilled a performer as she's proving herself to be, and within no time he'd undoubtedly let slip to me somehow that she's onto us. More likely, she's thinking of a way she can get herself and Elsie out of here.

I turn back to the window. The night is black, rain lashing against the window in an angry downpour. Driving conditions are awful. The lanes will be a nightmare; they're dangerous enough in the dark at the best of times, but no one would be mad enough to attempt them during a storm like this. Especially not with a young child in tow. It's just as well that for once the weather's exactly as the forecast predicted. No one is leaving the farm tonight.

THIRTY-SIX

Natalie goes past Elsie's room to get to her own. Jake and Elsie are sitting on the bed together, Elsie curled beneath his arm as he reads her a story. The sight of them together here like this stops her dead in her tracks. Since the moment she'd found out she was pregnant, this was all she'd wanted. A loving father for her child; a family man, like her own father. A happy home. It was everything she'd believed she and Jake had. Elsie wasn't planned, but when she'd found out she was pregnant, it seemed that history was happily repeating itself. She was not much older than her mother had been when she'd had Natalie, and when she thought of her parents, she was only able to recall contentment. They were fulfilled in their lives here. They must have had their problems, as every marriage does, yet as a child Natalie had never been exposed to them. She'd had a perfect childhood, and it was everything she had wanted for her daughter.

Now, when she gazes at the scene in the bedroom, all she sees is a lie. Their entire life here has been based on fabrication, all, it seems, because Jake's been too much of a coward to admit who he is and what he really wants. She's not the only victim in all this. How is Elsie going to react when she's older, when she finds out what happened here for so much time? Every truth has a way of making itself known eventually.

Jake stops mid-sentence and looks up from the story he's reading to Elsie. He smiles, and Natalie feels her stomach twist with the betrayal.

'Food's ready,' she tells him.

She goes to the bedroom to change, peeling off her wet jeans and pulling on a pair of comfy leggings from the wardrobe. Tonight, she'll play the role of doting wife and best friend. It will be the performance of a lifetime, and she knows it will take everything she has. She casts a last look at herself in the mirror, reminding herself of Kara's words. She can do this, she thinks. She must do it. Tomorrow, when she's able to, she will get Elsie from here. If Natalie tells her about Jake and Tyler, she's sure Holly's parents will put them up for a while, just long enough for her to find evidence of wrongdoing on Tyler's part. If Kara's claims are true, everything she needs is in May's house.

When Natalie goes downstairs to the kitchen, Jake and Elsie are already there, sitting at the table. Elsie's pushing a blob of mashed potato around her plate, prodding it every now and then like a jelly. Tyler's by the sink, opening a bottle of wine. He pours three glasses at the sink, his back kept turned to them. I know what you're doing, Natalie thinks. Now, she's able to see everything. How easy it's been for him to spike a beer here, a meal there; a cup of tea every time he's played the caring and considerate friend. How easy it was for him to drug her daughter with antibiotics.

'Thank you,' she says, swallowing down the urge to lunge at him as he places a glass in front of her. She's no intention of drinking it, or of eating anything either. When Tyler starts piling food onto her plate, she raises a hand. 'Not too much,' she says. 'I don't mean to be rude when you've gone to so much effort, but I've not been feeling well all afternoon.'

'Are you okay?' Jake asks.

Like you care, she wants to say, but instead she nods. 'Probably picked something up from Elsie.'

She watches her daughter shunt the food around her plate, relieved she doesn't seem to have eaten any either, and when Elsie pushes her plate away, Natalie could kiss her.

'I don't like it.'

Natalie watches Tyler's reaction, seeing the anger beneath the smile he wears so effectively. 'Don't worry, Elsie. I'll make you something else.'

'No,' Natalie says, too hurriedly. 'You've done enough. Sit down. I'll do her something.'

Tyler hesitates, but then sits down to join them. Natalie goes to the fridge and throws together a haphazard picnic for Elsie – a few squares of bread and butter, some carrot sticks, some cubes of cheese and some strawberries.

'Did you have a good day at nursery?' Tyler asks Elsie, as Natalie returns to the table with her food.

Elsie shoves a cube of cheddar into her mouth and says nothing. She should have seen it, Natalie thinks. Elsie's been so quiet around him, something Natalie had put down to confidence and delayed speech. But maybe there was more to it. Perhaps Elsie was able to see more than Natalie could. Now, she wonders what happened the night Tyler did bedtime with Elsie. Just what might he have said to her, what might he have done, to make her so cautious around him?

Midway through their meal, Jake gets up to use the toilet.

'You've barely touched your food,' Tyler says to Natalie, though she hasn't even eaten a mouthful.

'There's a sickness bug going around at the nursery,' she lies. 'I hope we don't come down with something by the morning.'

'No,' he says, looking up at her across the opened bottle of wine that sits in the middle of the table. 'We wouldn't want that.'

Elsie gets down from the table and goes to her toy kitchen. While she potters with plastic cups and saucers, Natalie grabs the bottle of wine, noticing that Jake's glass is nearly empty. 'Top up?' she says, after refilling Jake's glass, and then she realises Tyler's glass is still full. He hasn't touched a drop either. He's spiked the bottle.

When he returns from the bathroom, she notices Jake's speech is already slurred. He's only had one glass – not enough to have had this effect. She wants to move his glass away from him, but Tyler now seems to be watching her every move. She begins to panic, inwardly fighting the urge to get up from the table, grab Elsie and run from the house. They could go to Holly's house; her family doesn't live far. Yet even those few miles are too far in these conditions. The storm outside is the worst she's seen in years, having escalated faster than the forecast anticipated. She'd have no chance of making it far. Not far enough that Tyler wouldn't have time to catch up with them.

'It's getting late,' Natalie says, glancing at the clock above the microwave. 'I'm going to get Elsie to bed. Elsie, two minutes and we're going upstairs, okay?'

Elsie starts to groan and whinge.

'Elsie!' Natalie snaps.

The little girl looks at her mother in shock; Natalie rarely raises her voice and isn't prone to outbursts of frustration. Elsie's bottom lip starts to quiver and when she starts crying Natalie goes to her, wrapping her in a hug and telling her she's sorry.

'It's late, darling, that's all,' she tells her. 'Come on, let's go and pick a nice story to read.'

When she stands, Tyler is at the kitchen doorway. For a second Natalie thinks he's going to block their way and stop them from trying to leave, but then he steps towards her and puts his arms out, beckoning her towards him for a hug. It's all Natalie can do not to recoil from his touch. She raises her arms tentatively, returning the gesture of faked affection. She crosses her hands behind his neck and rests her head against his shoulder, her mind fleetingly filled with an image of herself squeezing her hands around his throat, forcing the breath from him.

'Thank you,' Tyler says. 'I mean it. You're the best.'

Her heart thuds so loudly in her chest she feels certain he must hear it. How can he stand here and play out a lie like this?

His mouth moves closer to her face as he speaks softly into her ear, his voice lowered to a whisper. 'Don't worry, I'll look after him for you.'

Natalie jolts from him at the words, but Tyler smiles as though they weren't just spoken.

'Night, night, Elsie,' he says. 'Sleep tight.'

THIRTY-SEVEN

'Don't be surprised if I don't make it back downstairs,' Natalie tells us, with mock apology, her reaction to my words still fixed on her features. 'I quite often fall asleep with her at bedtime.'

She's making an excuse so that she doesn't have to leave Elsie alone, not while I'm here. She doesn't trust me, and she's right not to. She'll no doubt stay in Elsie's bed with her, waiting for a chance to leave. I'm going to have to set things in motion before the storm begins to subside.

'Don't worry about anything,' I tell her. 'Look after that headache.'

I watch her leave and wait to hear their footsteps on the landing. When I look at Jake, he's slumped in his chair, his eyes already half closed.

'Why are you doing this?' he says.

He knows. He realises now that his drink was spiked, and when he tries to stand his feet give way beneath him. 'Woah,' I say, reaching to grab him before he falls. 'Easy. Someone can't handle their booze.'

When he looks at me, he looks through me, not knowing who he's seeing. He tries to claw at my face as I drag him to the kitchen door, desperately trying to fight me off him, but the drug has weakened him and he's barely able to keep his eyes open let alone put up any kind of resistance.

'Come on,' I tell him. 'Let's get you comfy.'

I half drag, half carry him through to the living room where I let him drop onto the sofa. He's already almost asleep; by the time he wakes, all this will be over. He'll know I did what was needed, what was best for us both.

I move him so he's comfortable and put a blanket over him.

'No one...' he manages to say, but he can't quite finish the sentence.

'Don't worry about anything,' I tell him, pushing hair that needs cutting back from his face. 'Everything's going to be okay.'

I sit on the carpet beside him for a while, studying his beautiful face as he struggles to keep his eyes open. Sometimes I think about what my life might have looked like if I hadn't stayed in Llanafon. I'd had opportunities, but I'd let them all go. For him. For us. For this place. I would have met someone else. There would have been plenty of other men, but no one like Jake. We come from the same place; we understand each other. But maybe really loving someone means having to let them go.

'I'm sorry,' I say, and I take his hand. 'But I gave you so much time. I gave you everything.'

Jake inhales sharply, fighting to get out the words he wants to say.

'No one was meant to get hurt.'

'Shhh,' I soothe, running the back of my hand across his forehead. 'Sleep it off. You'll be fine.'

I wait for him to slip into sleep before kissing him on the cheek and telling him I love him. It was true, once, though I'm less and less sure as time goes on. My mother might have been right, for once in her life.

I leave Jake sleeping and creep as quietly as I can up the stairs, but the house is old and the staircase is noisy, the floorboards creaking beneath every step. Natalie won't be asleep. She'll be in Elsie's bed, poised waiting for me, ready with the knife I saw her pull from the block on the kitchen worktop and slip under her jumper when she thought I was distracted with the cooking. The landing's as noisy as the stairs, and when I get to the bedroom doorway, it's shut fully. I push on the handle. There's something on the other side, blocking the door. Elsie's wardrobe, I'm guessing – not a full size one, but big enough. I shove the door once, twice, pressing all my weight on to it.

'I've called the police!' Natalie shouts. 'They're already on their way!'

Her attempts to disarm me are wasted. Her mobile phone is in the oven, where I put it earlier after taking it from her coat pocket, hiding it there so she wouldn't be able to find it. I cut the landline before she got back.

Elsie's woken and has started crying. I say nothing before slamming into the door again, this time feeling the weighty wardrobe move behind the door. It shifts on the next one, and I'm then able to put a hand in to force it back further. That's when a flame of searing pain rips through the back of my hand, and when I pull my arm back blood pumps from the wound she's sliced across my knuckles.

'You fucking bitch!'

Rage powers me, and I force myself through the gap in the door. Natalie charges at me like a wild animal in the half light, but I'm too quick for her. My right hand throbs, but with my left arm I'm able to knock the knife from her hand. It flips across the carpet somewhere, out of sight, and when I grab her around the throat she continues to grasp for it, fighting me with everything she's got. I hit her across the face so hard I split her lip. The violence comes as such a shock that for a moment it disables her; she falls limp in my hands, long enough for me to twist her arms behind her back and pull the rope from my pocket.

'Please,' she says, spitting blood with the word. 'Don't do this.'

'It's okay, Elsie,' I say, as the crying intensifies. 'Mummy and Uncle Tyler are just playing a game, okay?'

But Elsie isn't an idiot. She looks at her mother in terror as she presses herself against the wall, her duvet pulled to her raised knees as she cowers away from the scene unfolding in her bedroom.

I work a knot around Natalie's wrists, tying them together.

'Elsie,' Natalie says quietly, pleadingly. 'Run!'

Elsie tries to get up from the bed, but she gets herself tangled in her duvet. I pull the roll of duct tape I'd hidden in the kitchen earlier from my pocket and tape Natalie's mouth to shut up her screams, then I retrieve the knife from the carpet in the corner. Neither of them are leaving this room, not until I'm ready.

'Get back on the bed,' I tell Elsie, and when I hold the knife in front of me, she looks to her mother for confirmation that she should do as she's told. Being sensible for once, Natalie nods for her to listen. She cries as I tie her to the radiator, muffled pleas escaping from behind the tape.

She writhes in terror when I lift Elsie, screaming and crying from the bed.

'Don't worry,' I tell Natalie, leaning over her to wipe a streak of blood from her wet cheek. 'I'll be back for you.'

THIRTY-EIGHT

The more Natalie fights to free herself from the knots keeping her in Elsie's room, the weaker she finds she's becoming. Her mind strays to the darkest of places, imagining what Tyler's doing to Elsie, but the thought of her daughter is also what holds her in place, her focus on her hands, the pain that cuts through her wrists now a separate entity, not belonging to her. She tries to cry out, but the duct tape across her mouth blocks any sound, and the more panicked she becomes, the harder it is to breathe through her nose.

Calm down, she tells herself. She has to stay calm, for Elsie's sake.

She moves as close as she can to the set of drawers. It's too dark to make things out clearly enough, but she knows somewhere on top of the chest there's a jewellery box with some of Elsie's plastic necklaces, bracelets and hair accessories inside. She's pretty sure there's some metal hair pins in there too, and she hopes desperately that the nail scissors she used last week to cut Elsie's nails might be inside too.

She turns herself so that her back's against the drawers and then shoves herself against it. The chest wobbles, so she does it again, this time harder. Something falls and hits her on the shoulder, but as her eyes adjust to the dark she sees it's Elsie's nightlight. She manoeuvres her leg to raise her foot and press her heel to the button on top, activating the light. She can see the box now, but another shove against the drawers still isn't enough to bring it closer to the edge.

Natalie takes a deep breath, readying herself for another attempt. She pushes back thoughts of what might be happening to Elsie. Tyler is a liar and a cheat and possibly worse... but just how much worse, she doesn't want to consider, not now while he's somewhere with her child. She shoves the chest of drawers in a rage, and the box falls to the carpet, too far for her to be able to reach it.

Then she hears footsteps on the stairs. He's come back for her. She searches for something she can grab, but with her hands tied and nothing within reach of her feet now, she's helpless. She pulls her legs back, poised to kick Tyler when he gets close enough, but when she twists her body to see him enter the room, the silhouette in the doorway isn't his. Then Kara is lit by the glow of the nightlight.

'Natalie,' she says, rushing to her. 'Quick. We don't have much time.'

There are shears in her hands, and as Kara cuts through the rope that holds Natalie to the radiator, she cries with relief. Kara quickly rips the tape from her mouth.

'What are you doing here?' Natalie whispers.

'I said I wouldn't leave you while you needed me. I never break a promise.'

'Please, Kara. There's something you're not telling me.'

'Dougie Cartwright. The man who killed my sister. He's Tyler's brother. He's the reason I came here. There's too much to explain now, but I promise I will.'

Natalie flexes her fingers as her hands are released, working the blood and the life back into them. Her brain swells with Kara's words.

'He's taken Elsie to the barn,' Kara tells her, as she hands Natalie the shears. 'Hide these. Don't let him know I'm here.'

Natalie takes the shears and swallows her fear. 'Where are you going?'

'I'm not leaving you,' Kara promises. 'Just don't give me away, okay?'

She follows Natalie onto the landing but lingers near the bathroom when Natalie goes downstairs. Natalie passes the open living room door and she sees Jake asleep on the sofa. He probably won't stir now; the drugs in his drink, meant for her, were probably strong enough to keep him knocked out for hours. Long enough for Tyler to implement whatever sick plan he has in place. She should be concerned for him, she thinks, but in this moment, she doesn't care whether Jake's okay or not. He's brought all of this upon them, and now his selfishness has put their daughter's life in danger.

When she heads for the kitchen, Natalie hears Kara on the stairs. She goes out to the barns through the kitchen door, grabbing another knife on her way out, the shears still beneath her jumper. The storm is relentless, the force of the rain knocking her sideways as she steps from the house. The wind screams in her ear, and there's a clanging somewhere, a gate left opened, sounding out like a warning klaxon amid the chaos of the night.

Her heart pounds so hard she thinks it could overwhelm every other noise, enough to drown out the howling of the wind. She clutches the knife in her hand, her sleeve pulled as low as she's able to stretch it; she feels it now, shaking in her grip as she wills her fingers to stay steady. Then she sees a flash of light up ahead in the furthest barn, and she runs for it, panting as she tries to ready herself for whatever she may find there.

As she nears the barn, she sees movement in the crack of the open doorway. She treads carefully across the tarmac, legs like marshmallow beneath her. When she reaches the barn door, Tyler has his back to her. A torch is propped on the floor, shooting a glow towards him as he sets about his task. He's arranging hay bales into some kind of formation, and when her eyes adjust to the darkness, Natalie's breath escapes her. They're stacked in a pile, a sleeping Elsie placed on top like some sort of sacrificial offering. Then she sees the fireworks on the ground at his feet. The box of matches waiting close at hand.

THIRTY-NINE

I turn at the sound of a crack beneath a footstep to find Natalie in the barn doorway, her body an outline against the darkness. I watch as she takes in the details of my set-up: Elsie asleep on the pile of hay; the unused fireworks placed at the base. One lit match, that's all it takes.

'Why are you doing this?' she says, her voice barely a whisper amid the noise of the storm that drives on unforgivingly behind her. 'We've given you everything.'

'Not quite everything.'

She moves towards me. She's holding something in her hand, trying to conceal whatever it is beneath her sleeve. Another knife, I suspect. The pain in my hand throbs at the thought, but I've endured much worse than this, and I can do it all over again.

'Stop.' I grab the box of matches from the hay bale. 'Take another step and there'll be the biggest fireworks display you've ever seen.'

'Don't. Please.' Natalie looks at Elsie, her face fraught with panic. I see her wet eyes shimmering in the darkness, the fear

that runs through them strong enough to shine in the darkness.
'She's just a child. What have you done to her?'

'Nothing. She's sleeping, that's all.'

'I know about you and Jake. You can have him. You can
have the farm if it's what you want – you can take it all, I don't
care. Just don't hurt Elsie, Tyler. Please.'

She means it, but it's not as easy as that. I can't trust her. If I
let her go, I'll live a life spent looking over my shoulder, always
wondering when the knock at the door's going to come. Natalie
may think she means it now, but she'd never keep this secret
forever. Just like me, she won't let this place go without a fight.

'I loved you like a brother.'

'I loved you like a sister,' I reply. 'But I've never really been
a part of any of this, have I? Families are supposed to share.'

'So you thought you'd share my husband? How long has it
been going on, Tyler?'

I want to tell her. I want so badly to tell her that we were
fucking on her parents' sofa while she was at school; I want to
tell her that he's been mine for the past decade, that he was
always mine and was only ever on loan to her. I want to tell her
that I've always been the one who knows him better than
anyone. But where would all that get us now? I don't believe in
this moment that she cares for Jake any more than I do.

'You'll die a heroine, Natalie, just remember that. You sacrificed your own life to try to save your daughter. If people can
see past the negligence, that is. You know, leaving matches lying
around while there's a three-year-old in the house and a load of
unused fireworks in the barn. But everyone already knows how
careless you are. Anyway, you'll go down in local legend. Much
like your parents.'

'Don't bring them into this. If you'd ever thought anything
of them, you'd never be doing what you're doing now. They
treated you like a son.'

Her words provoke a reaction she couldn't have anticipated.

I feel fire burn through me; a rage so fierce it could light the night sky from here to the next village. I strike the match, and when Natalie rushes towards me, I hold it directly over the fuse end of the fireworks.

'Exactly. I was supposed to be a son to them, but what did they leave me with? Nothing. I'm as entitled to this place as you are. You don't know anything about running this farm beyond your little ice cream hobby. If it wasn't for Jake and me this place would've been run into the ground. You're nothing without us.'

'If you do this,' Natalie says, her voice shaking, 'the police will know. There'll be an investigation – they'll know all this was started deliberately. Why would Elsie climb on top of a pile of hay after accidentally starting a fire? She'd be running for the barn door, trying to escape. There'll be tests – they'll find whatever you've given her to make her sleep. No one will believe this was an accident. You'll go to prison, Tyler. But if you let us go, you'll get what you want. You'll get Jake. This place. It's all yours. I don't want any of it.'

My hand trembles above the fuses. 'They left me nothing. All their words, all their promises, but when it came to it, they wrote me out. Didn't I deserve more than that?'

'And what about Jake? Do you really love him, or are you just using him to get at me? How long has this been going on?'

'Ten years,' I say, because I owe her the truth of this, at least. 'I'd have done anything for him. I'd have killed for him. Of course I've loved him.'

The match is burning down to my fingers now, its heat scorching my fingertips. I should let it drop, but I can't bring myself to do it. I watch her reaction in the glow of the flickering light, my words crushing her as the charade of her whole adult existence comes crashing around her. Her life is a lie. Now we both know how it feels.

'If you ever loved him, you could never hurt him like this,'

Natalie tries to persuade me. 'He'll never forgive you if you hurt Elsie. Please, Tyler. Blow out the match.'

'Do you think I want to be doing this?' I tell her, feeling shamed by the pain that rips through me. 'I love this place more than anything. I don't want to watch everything we've built here destroyed. And I'm not the monster you probably think I am.' I pause and look her straight in the eye. 'I really don't want to hurt my own niece like this.'

And I watch and wait for the truth to hit her, everything she knows fractured in an instant, all her memories shattered into worthless pieces the way mine were. And I enjoy the moment more than I know I should.

FORTY

The words take shape in front of Natalie, but she can't make any sense of them.

'What are you talking about?' she says quietly, not really wanting the answer.

'Good old Tom. Friend to everyone, your dad. Salt of the earth kind of guy. My mother apparently thought so, anyway.'

Natalie shakes her head. She won't hear this; it isn't true. Whatever he's suggesting, he's a liar. He's already more than proven that.

She watches as the match burns itself out against the tips of his fingers, Tyler unflinching against its scorch.

'You've got to have wondered why he was so good to me?' Tyler says. 'I mean, I did. But then I figured he was just a decent, kind man. That there might still be some of them left in the world. But it makes more sense now, doesn't it? It was guilt, all of it. Duty.'

'You are not my father's son,' Natalie says, the words forced between gritted teeth. 'That's not who he was. Whatever your mother's told you, she's a liar.'

'I heard them together. The week before my dad killed

himself, I heard May and Tom in the living room when I got home from school. *When were you going to tell me*, that's what he said to her.'

'That could have referred to anything,' Natalie argues.

'That's what I tried to tell myself too. For all this time, actually. But then you look back and things start to add up, don't they? The generosity, the concern. The fact my father ended his own life ten days after that conversation.'

Kara's word's come flooding back to her in a rush of noise that fills Natalie's brain. Dougie Cartwright. Tyler's brother. If May has only one son, and if Edward really wasn't Tyler's father, then that means perhaps she's also connected. Maybe Tyler is telling the truth. Tom was father to them all.

But it can't be true. None of it makes any sense.

She watches as Tyler lights another match. 'I'm sorry, Natalie. But it was always going to come to this. Jake was never going to do anything to make things work for us all.'

From the corner of her eye, she sees movement behind him. She keeps her focus on him. 'It doesn't have to come to this,' she says, trying to keep him talking. 'There are always other ways. I'll sign over everything. We'll get all the paperwork written up, you can do this without turning yourself into a criminal.'

But you're already a criminal, she thinks. You're a liar and you've committed fraud; you've drugged people, willingly exposing them to danger. But she says none of it, not wanting to lose him now.

'I'm sorry, Natalie,' he says again, as though willing her to believe he means it.

She sees the shovel before she sees Kara. It is almost bigger than her, swung with the determination of someone who knows she's chancing her luck. It glances off the side of Tyler's head, catching him at the temple; it's enough to take his feet from under him, but not enough to knock him out. He staggers sideways, caught off-guard, then slumps against the barn wall, cursing with the pain. Kara is already on top of the pile of hay now, bundling Elsie into her arms.

'Take her!' Natalie shouts. 'Run!'

The lit match has fallen to the ground near the fireworks. It's caught on the hay and she knows it won't be long before the place becomes a bonfire.

She follows Kara as she races for the barn door. Elsie's a rag doll in her hands, her limbs flopping loosely as Kara rushes her outside. Natalie turns to see Tyler already staggering upright again. She makes it to the barn door, but Kara and Elsie have disappeared in the darkness, either back in the house or somewhere out here in the storm, hidden from sight. Amid the pounding of the rain on the barn roof she can already hear the fizzing of the firework fuses. She slams the door shut, but Tyler's already at the other side, forcing it back against her. The wind screams in her ears as she uses all her weight to press against the door while she fumbles in the darkness for the padlock. She can't let him get out of here. If she does, he'll kill them all.

She hears him grunt as he forces the door open. Like a wild bull, he throws himself at the other side, the barn door bursting open and knocking her to the ground. He staggers above her as her eyes adjust to the darkness, the rain half blinding her. There's enough light from the moon for Natalie to make out the blood on the side of his face. Enough to see the deadness that lies behind his eyes. There's a groan and a creak overhead, and when Tyler reaches down to grab her by the leg, Natalie screams with all the energy she has left inside her.

The first firework goes off; she hears it screech through the barn before a second sets off with a bang that echoes across the fields and into the night. Tyler drags her across the ground, her face tearing on the grit as she writhes to free herself from his grip. Her head hits something, dazing her, and when she looks up she sees the shadow of the horse chestnut tree hanging over them. Rain continues to batter her face. She draws her free leg up to her stomach, and when she lowers it, she aims straight for the back of his knees.

Tyler crumples. The injury from the car accident has given him a lifelong weakness in his right leg and, without seeing the assault coming, he has nothing to stop himself from falling to the ground. He drops Natalie's leg as he collapses with the pain. She hears the groan again, this time directly above them. She scrambles in the dirt, trying to steady herself to gain her footing. The barn's caught fire, the pile of hay where Elsie lay just moments ago now a golden orb framed by the barn doors. The smell fills the air, acrid and heavy.

She hears another crack that fires like a gunshot. But she knows this is no firework. There's a scream so harrowing it chills her blood, and when she looks up she sees one of the lower branches falling, crashing with a thud to the ground beside her.

Tyler's cries ring out through the wind and the rain. 'Natalie! Help me!'

He lies beneath the branch, its weight crushing his legs.

'Natalie!' he cries out again. 'Please!'

She looks up at the darkened shape of the tree against the black night sky. Its trunk is split where it began to rot months ago, and against the force of the storm, one half pulls away from the other, shifting precariously, its structure groaning as it struggles to keep a hold.

'Kara!' she calls. 'Kara!'

She runs for the house, but Kara makes it outside first, Elsie no longer with her.

'Call for help!' Natalie screams.

She returns to Tyler, who's crying in pain beneath the branch, desperately trying to drag his body from under its weight. One or both legs must be broken, she thinks, the weakness that was already there from the accident making him vulnerable to injury. The branch is big, much larger than it looked up in the tree, but she's strong enough to move it. She is strong enough to drag him away.

The wind shrieks in her ears, rain lashing at her face as she looks down at him.

'It's going to go,' he cries, his voice desperate and pathetic as he watches the split in the tree trunk widen.

Natalie steps closer and crouches beside him. 'I know,' she says, then she leans to his ear, lowering her voice to a whisper. 'But don't worry, I'll look after him for you.'

She turns and walks away, and as she nears the house a single scream cuts through the noise of the storm. With an echoing crunch, the tree yields beneath its force and crashes to the ground. Natalie turns back to the flames and the downpour, searching for Tyler. But there's nothing but the machine-gun round of fireworks, the burst of flames as more hay ignites, and the noise of the pounding rain as it continues to hammer the earth relentlessly.

FORTY-ONE

When I wake, the first face I see is Natalie's. As my eyes adjust to the light, I realise I'm in a hospital room. Everything comes rushing back in a flood that threatens to drown me. The pain in my leg sears through my body, and I wince as I try to push myself up. Natalie's sitting in the chair by the bedside, her frail frame wrapped beneath a thin blanket. Her eyes are resting on my face, and I wonder how long she's been sitting there watching me, waiting for me to wake up.

Her eyes are red-rimmed and raw with crying. Those tears can't all have been for me.

'Oh, Tyler,' she says, our eyes meeting as mine struggle to focus. 'Thank God.'

She reaches forward and clasps my hand in hers. Her grip's so tight I feel my fingers weaken as she almost cuts off my circulation.

'Tom?' I manage, my voice weak. 'Jayne?'

Natalie shakes her head as she looks away, unable to speak the words. A sob bursts from her as a nurse comes into the room. She looks at Natalie with concern as she checks my file. 'Still here, love? Are you sure there's no one I can call for you?'

Natalie shakes her head again. 'No. Thank you.'

She sits back and waits silently as the nurse continues her work, keeping her head lowered to hide her face. I wonder whether she's been allowed to see her mother's and father's bodies. I wonder where they are now. I close my eyes. Still, even now, I can hear Jayne screaming from the back seat, her accusation ringing like an echo in my ear. *How could you? How could you? How could you?*

We should have been more careful. Jake and I should have stayed away from each other while we were on the farm. But we couldn't keep our hands off each other and it was dangerous, doing it where we knew we might get caught. It was part of the excitement.

Neither of us had heard Jayne at the barn door. She hadn't let on that she was there, and it was only when Tom offered to take me for a driving lesson that I found out what she'd seen. The driving lesson was just an excuse to get me on my own, somewhere they could talk to me without Natalie or Jake overhearing. They were going to tell her everything, they said. But not yet. Not before she'd finished her exams. They weren't going to jeopardise everything she'd worked so hard for. Their girl was going places, and nothing was going to put a stop to that.

'I thought we'd lost you too,' she says, finally letting go of my fingers. 'What happened, Tyler?'

She doesn't really want to know what happened. Details of the crash are the last thing she needs to hear. I say nothing; instead, I sit up, wincing with the pain that shoots through my leg.

'It's broken,' she says, her gaze following mine. 'Don't try to move it.' She reaches to take my hand in hers again. 'What happened?' she asks again, this time more insistent.

'I can't remember,' I lie. 'It was raining so hard.'

It all came to me so quickly. It suddenly all seemed clear –

so vivid that I was able to see those next few moments play out in front of me like a film reel. I knew what would happen. Jake was going to leave. He was going to follow Natalie to Nottingham, where they'd start a new life together. Once they were gone, they'd never come back. He'd live a new life without me. He'd live a lie. I would lose my job at the farm now Natalie's parents knew about Jake and me. Tom and Jayne would disown me. Everything I'd worked for would be for nothing.

But there was a way I could put it all right. A way I could make Natalie stay. And I could keep some kind of hold over the farm until I could work out how to make the place mine. If something were to happen to Tom and Jayne, Natalie wouldn't leave. I've known her long enough to know the person she is, and loyalty would keep her here, bound to her parents' legacy. Plus she'd never be able to study for a degree if she was consumed by grief. She'd stay where she is, bound by duty. But she wouldn't be able to do everything by herself. She'd need help running the farm. Jake and I would do it. The farm would keep us together.

I put my foot down hard on the accelerator. The louder Jayne became, the easier it all seemed. Rage descended in a mist on the lane in front of me. I'd already lost my dad. I wasn't going to lose Jake and the farm as well. And so I accelerated harder. Jayne screamed at me. Tom told me to slow down. He tried to grab the wheel. I saw the tree as we turned a bend, and I aimed straight for it. The bonnet crumpled. Tom hit the windscreen. In the back, Jayne fell silent. I'm not sure, but I don't think she'd been wearing a seat belt.

The next few moments passed as though I was living them in a dream. It wasn't really me who dragged Tom's body across the handbrake to slump him in the driver's seat. It wasn't me who found a rock at the roadside big enough to smash the driver's window from inside, and when I sliced my cheek with a shard of broken glass it was like watching someone who looked much like me, my real self lifted from my body. I had to make it look as though Tom had been driving, and all the while the pain in my leg seared through my body, removed from me for those moments, as though it didn't really belong to me.

The next vehicle to come along the road was a white van. The driver found me hanging out of the car from the passenger seat, a puddle of vomit on the tarmac. I hadn't needed to fake it: the pain was so bad by that point that the sickness was real. I knew the man; he was the uncle of a kid in the year below us, and he stayed with me until the ambulance arrived, talking to me to keep me awake while we both ignored the subject of the dead couple lying just behind me inside the car.

'What are we going to do?' Natalie sobs.

'I don't know,' I tell her. 'But I'll always be here for you, Natalie. You know that.'

The door opens. Jake bursts into the room, rain-soaked and grey-faced. He stops abruptly when he sees me in the bed, before his eyes roam to Natalie. He goes to her and puts his arms around her, smoothing her hair as she cries on his shoulder, and when I watch him kiss her face I'm forced to swallow down the jealousy I'm going to have to learn to control.

'I'm so sorry,' he says, speaking the words into her hair. Then he lifts his head and looks at me over her shoulder, and when his eyes meet mine his apology is silently repeated. *I love you*, he silently mouths at me, and my chest fills with something I've never been able to describe with words. All the pain I feel is justified; every inch of it is worth it. I would do it all again, a hundred times over, if it means keeping him here with me, because there is nothing I won't do to make Jake mine.

FORTY-TWO

She sees Jake's van as he pulls onto the driveway, and she goes outside to meet him. He already looks different to when she last saw him just a couple of weeks ago, first at May's funeral and then at Tyler's. The day after Tyler died, May had been found dead in her bed. Afterwards, Natalie realised that when she'd gone there that afternoon and had no reply, Tyler must have already been there. He had suffocated his mother with a pillow, the post-mortem showing evidence that she had put up a fight against him. She'd known her own son was the person who would end her life.

Natalie and Jake were amid just a handful of people who bothered to show up for Tyler's funeral, though May's had seen the whole village out in mourning. It seemed a tragedy to Natalie that May was so popular in death when she'd led such a life of solitude for all the years after her husband's death. She's wondered whether anyone else in the village had known about her affair with Tom all those years ago, if Tyler's claims were in fact true. It seems impossible that no one would have caught hold of their secret, although she reminds herself that only May had known of Tyler's and Jake's.

Jake looks older somehow, and he's lost weight. She didn't recognise him for a moment, but then she never really knew him, did she?

Most of his things have already been taken from the house; after today there will be nothing of him left here. He doesn't know she's already seen an estate agent about selling up, but he must realise there's no way she can stay. The foundations of her life here have been built on lies, and Jake doesn't deserve to keep the place. She doubts very much that he would want to, not now, after everything that's happened here.

Kara's going to return to university to continue her law course. She has already contacted the course leader who's confirmed a place will still be open to her. It's given Natalie renewed hope for the future. Perhaps, one day, she might also be able to pick back up the life she'd left behind.

'How are you?' Jake asks.

'Surviving. You?'

'Just about.'

He follows her into the house. Though they've seen each other before today, until now there have always been other people there. He hasn't yet had a chance to speak with her alone – she'd hoped to put that off for as long as she was able. But they both need closure. Once the house has been emptied and sold they can both move on with their lives, whatever those lives may now look like.

'Where's Elsie?' he asks, looking around the living room door.

'With Kara.'

She sees the reaction he tries to conceal. Resentment. He hadn't wanted her in their lives, and now she realises why. He was scared of his secret being found out, terrified an outsider might see more than Natalie was able to. And now their daughter's playing happily with Kara while Jake comes here to pack up the remainder of his life, a man broken by his own lies and deceit.

'How's she doing?'

'She's okay, everything considered. I mean, she's confused. She's wondering where her daddy and her Uncle Tyler are.'

Jake's eyes shimmer, but Natalie can't feel any sympathy for him. He'd had years to admit to his affair and, though it would have been too late for them whenever he'd told her, an earlier admission might have spared Elsie so much. Tyler and May needn't have died. Things could have been so different for them all.

'What am I supposed to tell her?'

Jake shakes his head. 'I don't know. I never meant for any of this to happen.'

'But what did you think was going to happen? You must have known that the longer it all went on, the worse things were going to be?'

'I don't know what I thought. The longer it went on, the harder it became to even think about telling you. How was I going to just drop something like that into conversation? I knew you'd hate me. I knew you'd take Elsie away from me.'

'Like I'm doing now?' she says. 'You'll always be her dad, Jake. But one day she's going to ask what happened, and you'll have to tell her. You'll owe her that.'

'Have social services been in touch?'

'Everything's been dropped. They know now Tyler was responsible for everything.'

She sees the guilt as it settles over Jake's face. If anyone should have seen what Tyler was doing, it should have been him.

'Did you know it was Tyler who'd given Elsie those antibiotics?'

Jake looks crushed by the question. 'Of course not. Christ, Natalie, what do you think I am?'

'That's the point. I don't know.'

'If I'd known for a minute—'

'You must have had some idea. That rewritten will he'd tricked me into signing—'

'I didn't know anything about that at the time.'

'At the time,' Natalie repeats, her eyebrow raised. 'So you knew something later on?'

'He told me you were letting him buy you out. That you were planning to leave me. I realise now it was all bullshit, but I didn't know what to believe at the time. Things were all over the place between us.'

Jake sinks into silence, and all Natalie sees when she looks at him is guilt. Were they planning on taking the place together? she wonders. Perhaps Tyler had built an imagined future for them here, in the same way she had. Jake must have realised Tyler's ambition was dangerous. The thought sends a sliver of doubt snaking through her. She won't let Elsie see him alone. Jake can have supervised access; she doubts he'll object to that, not while his affair with Tyler's still a secret from the rest of the village. Everyone knows that he killed his mother now, and that he attempted to murder Kara too. If people find out Jake was sleeping with him, they'll assume him guilty by association.

'If I'd thought for a second he'd do anything to hurt Elsie, I swear I would have ended things.'

But Natalie can't believe anything he tells her any more.

'He'd been drugging me as well,' she tells him. 'Did you know that? And the crow on the doorstep, the dead fuse in the freezer. It was all him, wasn't it? Did you know?'

Jake shakes his head vehemently. 'I swear to you, I didn't know a thing. On Elsie's life, Natalie, I swear to you.'

She opens the drawer of the hallway table and takes out the photo album she found a week earlier while she was clearing through some of their things. She hands it to him. 'Remember this?'

He takes it from her but he doesn't open it. He doesn't need to; he knows what's inside. Natalie made it for him as a gift for their first-year anniversary together, when they were just fifteen. Photographs from parties, train tickets from days out together; mementos of silly things that meant nothing to anyone except them. Now, she wonders whether any of them had ever meant anything to him.

'Was I just a smokescreen?'

'You were never that.'

'Of course I was. But you're too much of a coward to admit it even now.'

Jake looks down at the closed album.

'You could have told me then,' she says, jabbing a finger at the book. 'You could have spared us all so much.'

She's had plenty of time to consider this. Had he told her when they were teenagers that he was attracted to boys, it would have split her world in two. But she would have moved on; she would have had to. Now, she feels as though her entire adult life has been a lie. Their marriage was a sham, and she was kept in the dark like an idiot, something she doesn't know whether she'll ever be able to forgive him for.

'Why did you never just tell someone?'

'Who would I have told?' he says. 'My parents? They already knew; that's why they wanted nothing to do with me.' He watches Natalie's expression as it grows dark. 'Not about me and Tyler,' he corrects himself quickly. 'They never knew about us. I just mean they knew I...'

Natalie watches him struggle, still unable to say the words. In some other life, at some other time, she might have felt sorry for him. How trapped he must have felt to never have been able to say who he was and what he really wanted.

'And all this time you let me think it was because of me,' she says flatly. 'Every time I suggested we ask them over, for Elsie's sake, so she at least had one set of grandparents, you let me think they didn't want to know us because they didn't approve of me. You let me think that, in their eyes, I'd held you back. And I lived with that guilt all these years.'

'I'm sorry.'

'Don't even say it, Jake. It's meaningless now.' The fingers of her right hand squeeze those of her left as she wills herself not to get upset in front of him. 'Do you think he loved you back? He might have been infatuated with the idea of you and him, but that's not the same thing. I loved you, Jake. I gave you everything. Tyler just wanted to get his hands on the farm.'

Natalie doesn't really know whether all of this is true, but she can tell from Jake's reaction that the thought must have tormented him for these past couple of weeks, making him reassess everything he thought he'd known in the same way she's had to. Their wedding had been a rushed one: Jake had proposed to her in the June, and they'd been married by October. They didn't need the big fuss, he'd told her, and they couldn't afford it anyway. It would be romantic; they didn't need all the ceremony and tradition. They'd had a stranger as a witness when Tyler had called at the last minute to say there was an emergency with his mother and he wouldn't make it there in time. Jake and Natalie had both known it was an excuse, and at the back of her mind Natalie had secretly wondered whether Tyler just hadn't been able to watch her marry someone else. How wrong she'd got everything.

'Did you ever love me?' she asks him.

'Of course I did,' he says, but the pause before it is too long.

The past tense still manages to bruise her, though of course she knows any love he felt for her must have been consigned to history years ago. Way before Elsie was born, even. And it's this thought that burns with a greater intensity than any other.

'Were you in love with him?'

She doesn't expect a response to this, and she already knows what the answer is. Jake was blind to who Tyler really was in the same way she was blind to Jake, deluded by a love he'd grown up with. She suspects that despite everything Tyler was, he must have loved Jake at some point – or believed he did, at least.

She contemplates telling Jake what Tyler told her in the barn that night but decides to hold it back. No one needs to know. One day, maybe, she may try to find out, though she's not sure that with Tyler, May and Tom all gone it'll even be possible. Unless, of course, Dougie Cartwright holds the answer.

'I'll go and get the rest of my things. I'm so sorry, Natalie. For everything. I wish I'd done things differently.'

'Yeah. Me too.'

FORTY-THREE

Later, after Jake has left, Kara returns to the farm with Elsie. Natalie makes them dinner while Elsie watches television, and Kara joins her in the kitchen. She puts a box on the table before getting herself a drink.

'Thanks for taking Elsie out.'

'It was no problem. She's so lovely.'

Natalie smiles sadly. She worries how much all of this might affect Elsie long-term. She must have seen and registered so much more than Natalie will ever know.

'There's something I need to show you.'

Natalie glances at the box on the table. She's known this was coming, but she still isn't prepared for it. She's had enough to process over these past few weeks, and Kara has thankfully spared her. Natalie had asked for time to get through the funerals and to deal with her separation from Jake, and Kara had afforded her that. Her secret had already waited long enough; a few weeks more would make no difference.

But Kara's leaving soon, and the truth won't stay hidden forever.

Natalie goes with her to the table, and they sit side by side.

'Ready?'

'As ready as I'll ever be.'

Kara lifts the lid off the box and takes out a scrapbook. 'Tyler lived with you here for a while in twenty-ten, didn't he?'

'Yes. While May was in rehab.'

Kara shakes her head. 'She wasn't in rehab. She was helping Dougie Cartwright get away with murder.'

She opens the scrapbook and passes it to Natalie. There are details of legal documents that make little sense to her. Witness statements. There is Dougie's name. And then there is May's.

'I knew there was something corrupt going on. It never went to trial, even though Dougie was charged. There was evidence he'd been at the house when Hayley died, when he'd claimed he hadn't been. There was enough evidence from the post-mortem to suggest she hadn't simply lost her footing at the top of those stairs. Yet all of a sudden, the case was closed. May gave him an alibi. When I looked more into her background and found out where she was from, I couldn't understand why Dougie had chosen her to represent him. And why would she lie for him? Then I realised he hadn't chosen her. There was a man I'd seen them both with. I found out later who he was.'

Natalie hears her father's name before Kara speaks it.

'I'm sorry. I know none of this is what you want to hear. And I know you still don't believe me. But look.'

Kara reaches over to take back the scrapbook. It's a mosaic of photographs and newspaper cuttings, internet print-offs and handwritten notes. It is years of commitment and obsession. A sister's love. A promise to find the truth.

Finding the page she's looking for, Kara hands the book back to Natalie. 'Here,' she says, pointing to a faded copy of a photograph. It shows a group of teenagers gathered by a hotel pool bar, all dressed in swimwear, all holding cocktails as they pull faces for the camera.

'Ibiza,' Kara tells her. 'Nineteen ninety-one.'

Natalie studies the photograph carefully, scanning each face in turn. Then she sees him, recognisable when she looks closely enough to the details of the jaw line and the cheeky smile. Her father, Tom. She does the mental maths to work out how old he would have been when the photograph was taken. Nineteen. Two years after he'd met her mother.

In the photograph, Tom stands with his arm around a young woman wearing a bikini, his hand resting lightly on her bare hip.

'Jessica Cartwright,' Kara tells her, reading Natalie's thoughts. 'Dougie was born nine months after this photograph was taken.'

She knows she's supposed to feel something, yet Natalie remains numb. So much has been thrown at her over those past few months that this now seems weightless, that it might ricochet off the protective armoury she has built around herself.

'But why would May help Dougie? Why would she have jeopardised her own career like that?'

'She didn't do it for Dougie. She did it for Tom. And I'm presuming Tom did it out of guilt. Or maybe Jessica threatened to tell your mother about Dougie if Tom didn't help them out. We'll never know now.'

When Natalie turns the page, Kara doesn't try to stop her. Her own face looks back at her. Facebook profile pictures. Photographs taken from the farm's page. Then there is Tyler. Jake.

'I saw your advertisement for a room through the farm's Facebook page. I'd set up a fake account and started following you a few years back, once I found out Tyler worked here.'

'You came here for him?'

'For him. For May.'

Natalie meets her eye. If all this is true, she came here for her too.

'You're not your father's daughter,' Kara reassures her. 'I

knew that very quickly after meeting you. I wanted to hate you, but I couldn't.'

'You didn't need to take revenge,' Natalie says, passing back the book. 'Tyler did it all for you.'

The car crash, Natalie thinks. May's murder. Tyler inadvertently did all the dirty work, so Kara didn't have to.

Kara closes the book and puts it on the table. 'I'm so sorry, Natalie.'

'Don't be. I'm grateful to you, for everything.'

'You've nothing to thank me for,' Kara tells her. 'If anything, I sometimes wonder whether you were right. Your life would have been simpler if I'd never arrived here.'

'And as you said before, I'd have been living a lie. You arrived in my life just when you were needed. I might have lost everything if it wasn't for you. I might have lost Elsie.'

Kara puts a hand on her arm. 'None of this was your fault. You're not responsible for what any of them did. It must have been difficult seeing Jake, just the two of you.'

'I think he blames me. You know, for Tyler's death.'

'You mustn't feel guilty,' Kara tells her. 'You weren't to blame. You tried to save him.'

They are interrupted by Elsie, who comes into the kitchen carrying two conkers on strings. 'Co-comes!' she says proudly, dangling them like pendulums in either hand.

'Where did you find those?' Natalie asks, trying to remember where she'd put them when she'd drilled the holes in weeks ago. She'd intended to show Elsie how to play with them, but they'd never got around to it.

She watches as Elsie gets the strings tangled together then gets frustrated when she's unable to unwind them.

'Here.' She reaches for the conkers and takes the knot of string from Elsie. 'I'll show you how to play it.' She undoes the tangle and passes one of the conkers to Kara.

'You have a conker each, and you hit them against each

other until one of you takes out the other. Sometimes, if one of them is rotten inside, you can knock it down in one big hit.'

She looks across and meets Kara's eye, a moment of silence stretching between them. She doesn't need to speak a word for Kara to hear the admission.

'I had time,' she admits. 'There was enough time for me to move h—'

'Stop it,' Kara admonishes her. 'I won't say a word. And I never break a promise... you already know that.' She beckons Elsie over to her. 'Can you go and get Loulou for me?'

They watch Elsie run from the room, clacking the conkers against each other as she leaves.

'You've trusted me with your secret,' Kara says. 'And now I'm going to trust you with mine. Tyler didn't kill May... I did. And when Dougie Cartwright gets out of prison, I'm going to kill him too.'

A LETTER FROM VICTORIA

Dear Reader,

I'd like to say a massive thank you for choosing to read *Happily Married*. I can't quite believe that I'm now writing my twelfth thank you letter, and I am so grateful to everyone who has read my books, written reviews, and taken the time to share on social media. Six years ago, when I signed my first contract, I would never have imagined that I would still be here twelve books on, and this wouldn't have been possible without your ongoing support.

If you enjoyed *Happily Married* and would like to keep up to date with all my latest releases, just sign up at the following link. Your email address will never be shared, and you can unsubscribe at any time.

www.bookouture.com/victoria-jenkins

This story had sat with me for quite a while before I started writing; I could see the setting of the farm as clearly as though I knew the place, and the characters introduced themselves like long-lost friends. I love to read psychological thrillers with claustrophobic settings and a small cast of characters in which everyone is potentially untrustworthy, and with this book I wanted to achieve the kind of 'what did I just read?' moment that would have readers turning back through the pages to reconsider everything they thought they'd known. I really hope I've achieved this.

I hope you've enjoyed the different relationships portrayed in the story. For me, Tyler's and Jake's relationship was a true love story – to begin with, at least – but one doomed to fail – first at the hands of unaccepting parents and the boys' own fears, and later at the high price of Tyler's greed. Despite all his weaknesses and poor decisions, I hope Jake remains to some extent a sympathetic character – a young man trapped by circumstances, many of which were beyond his control. But above all else, this story for me is one of female solidarity and an unlikely bond – of how two strangers' lives can come together by chance (or seemingly so) and how both can, in different ways, 'save' the other.

I hope you loved reading *Happily Married* as much as I loved writing it; if so, I would be very grateful if you could write a review. I love to hear your thoughts, and they really do make a difference in helping new readers to discover my books for the first time.

I love hearing from readers – you can get in touch through my Facebook page or on Twitter.

Thank you,

Victoria

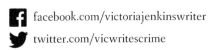

facebook.com/victoriajenkinswriter
twitter.com/vicwritescrime

ACKNOWLEDGEMENTS

The biggest thank you to my editor, Helen Jenner, who loved this book from the first read and has once again been an absolute pleasure to work with. Thank you for your enthusiasm and for taking all the loose ends and making the story complete. I feel very lucky to work with you and the rest of the team at Bookouture. I will be forever grateful that you made my dream a reality.

To Noelle and all the rest of the publicity team, thank you for your ongoing support and your seemingly endless energy. Thank you also to my agent, Anne Williams, who championed this book from the first read and has been an invaluable support to me and my writing.

Thank you to my family for continuing to encourage and support me while I spend half my time in a world of make-believe with my imaginary friends (Kate, when you tell me I've 'gone again' because I'm 'doing the face', this is where I've disappeared). To my lovely little girls, Mia and Emily, who don't believe I have a proper job – thank you for being you, and for making me a better me. There is a little bit of you two somewhere in everything I write, and you are always the sunshine in the darkness.

To my friends, Emma Tallon and Casey Kelleher, thank you for making me a little darker (you were right... a broken fuse was never going to be badass enough). Our Gladstone Library trips seem now to be where I produce my best work, and that's partly the space and time but mostly you girls – you make me feel a more capable version of myself, and women like you are the best type of friends to have. Emma, thank you for the 'mic drop' line... you'll know it when you see it.

A massive thank you to Caryl Phillips, who advised me about living and working on a dairy farm. I am in awe of everything you manage to do and achieve while raising three young children, and I am incredibly grateful to you for taking the time to share your experiences and the ins and outs of your daily life. Thank you, also, to my beta reader, Julie Clement – the first eye to spot the things that seemed clear to my mind but wouldn't have made any sense to anyone else.

My last and biggest thank you is to Steve. I learned a lot from you fifteen years ago about self-belief, and I continue to learn now. Thank you for supporting me – I couldn't write a page without you.